Selected Stories by
A.A. MILNE

Books in this Series:

Selected Stories by
A.A. MILNE

RUPA

Published by
Rupa Publications India Pvt. Ltd 2015
7/16, Ansari Road, Daryaganj
New Delhi 110002

Sales Centres:
Allahabad Bengaluru Chennai
Hyderabad Jaipur Kathmandu
Kolkata Mumbai

ISBN: 978-81-291-3721-0

First impression 2015

10 9 8 7 6 5 4 3 2 1

Printed at Repro Knowledgecast Limited, Thane

CONTENTS

INTRODUCTION

Alan Alexander Milne (18 January 1882–31 January 1956), better known as A. A. Milne, was an English author, best remembered for his creation of the character Winnie-the-Pooh, widely loved by children.

While Milne wrote poetry, short stories, plays and essays on many subjects, he is most famous for two poetry collections for children, *When We Were Very Young* and *Now We Are Six*, and the storybooks *Winnie-the-Pooh* and *The House at Pooh Corner*. The Pooh books were based on his son Christopher Milne and his teddy bear Edward, who in the books was called Winnie-the-Pooh.

Milne wrote for the literary magazine *Punch* from 1906 to 1914. He penned numerous essays and short stories whose tone was generally sarcastic and funny. Milne served as an officer in the British army in World War I and later in his life wrote three non-fiction books on war and pacifism, *Peace with Honour*, *War with Honour*, and *War Aims Unlimited*, as well as the autobiography *It's Too Late Now: The Autobiography of a Writer*, and the essay collection *Year in, Year out*.

The stories and essays collected here show Milne's mastery over language that allows him to weave witty tales around ordinary, everyday events.

- Told as a story narrated to a young niece, 'The King's Sons' is a fairytale with a twist.
- 'The Same Old Story' is a humourous story about a parrot named Evangeline and the attempt to teach her to speak.
- In 'The First of Spring' the narrator, fancying himself an expert gardener, sets about preparing the garden for the coming of spring.
- 'Afternoon Sleep' is a story about the narrator's niece, Margery, as he tries desperately to take an afternoon nap while also trying to humour the young child.
- 'Wrongly Attributed' is a humourous piece about a neighbour practising the piano and the agonies it causes the narrator.
- 'The Birthday Present' recounts a funny conversation between the narrator and his wife about a birthday present for her.
- 'Crown of Sorrows' is a humorous story about the narrator losing his precious hat in a music hall.
- 'My Secretary' is another one of Milne's stories starring the narrator's young niece, Margery, and the letters she wrote him.
- 'The Art of Conversation' is yet another story about Margery's antics and her uncle's valiant efforts to keep her occupied.
- 'Bachelor Relics' is a humorous story about selling old relics.
- 'Chapter of Accidents' is a hilarious account of a pair of young men going to visit a friend and how that ends up.
- 'The Doctor' is a humorous story about medical etiquette.
- 'Enter Bingo' is a story about an adorable Pekinese puppy named Bingo.
- 'The Fatal Gift' is the story of a lost cigar case and the unfortunate consequences of finding it.
- 'The Complete Kitchen' is a story about the narrator learning to play a game called 'Furnishing a Kitchen'.

- 'Getting Married' is a timeless account of the travails of arranging a wedding.
- In 'Pooh Gets Stuck in Rabbit's Hole' Pooh has to go on a diet to be pulled out of a hole he is stuck in.
- 'Tiggers Don't Climb Trees' is an adventure starring Tigger, the tiger, and Roo, the kangaroo.
- 'Pooh and Piglet Go Hunting and Nearly Catch a Woozle' is another story about the lovable Winnie-the-Pooh and his friend Piglet.
- 'Winnie-the-Pooh and Some Bees' is a short story about Winnie-the-Pooh's love for honey and how that gets him into trouble, again.
- In 'The Ordeal by Water' the narrator is coerced by a friend to bathe in the sea early in the morning, much against his will.
- 'The Adventurer' is the story of a nefarious conman and the amusing way in which he makes his fortune.
- 'A Breath of Life' recounts how a play ends unexpectedly on its opening night owing to its lovelorn leading actor.
- 'Chum' is a lovely story starring a loving dog and his master, which any pet owner will relate to.
- 'Common' is a heartwarming story about a toy dog and how he becomes a lucky mascot for his owner.
- 'Definitions' is a story about a parlour game.
- 'Getting the Needle' is a story about the strange knack the star of the story has for finding a hidden needle blindfolded.
- 'The Handicap of Sex' is a sympathetic take on women always having to assume the role of listeners.
- 'The Lucky Month' is a satirical story about astrology and one's birth month.

1

THE KING'S SONS

'Tell me a story,' said Margery.
'What sort of a story?'
'A fairy story, because it's Christmas-time.'
'But you know all the fairy stories.'
'Then tell me a new fairy story.'
'Right,' I said.

Once upon a time there was a King who had three sons. The eldest son was a very thoughtful youth. He always had a reason for everything he did, and sometimes he would say things like 'Economically it is to the advantage of the State that—' or 'The civic interests of the community demand that—' before doing something specially horrid. He didn't want to be unkind to anybody, but he took what he called a 'large view' of things; and if you happened to ask for a third help of plum-pudding he took the large view that you would be sorry about it next morning—and so you didn't have your plum-pudding. He was called Prince Proper.

The second son was a very wise youth. You couldn't catch him anyhow. If you asked him whether he knew the story of the three wells, or 'Why does a chicken cross the road?' or anything really amusing like that, he would always say, 'Oh, I heard that years ago!'—and whenever you began 'Adam and Eve and Pinchme' he would pinch you at once without waiting like a gentleman until you had got to the end of the verse. He was called Prince Clever.

And the third son was just wonderfully beautiful. He had the most marvellously pink cheeks and long golden hair that you have ever seen. I don't much care for that style myself, but in the country in which he lived it was admired more than I can tell you. He was called Prince Goldenlocks. I'll give you three guesses why.

Now the King had reigned a long time, so long that he was tired of being king, and he often used to wonder which of his sons ought to succeed him. Of course, nowadays they never wonder, and the eldest son becomes king at once, and quite right too; but in those days it was generally left to the sons to prove which among themselves was the most worthy. Sometimes they would all be sent out to find the magic Dragon's Tooth, and only one would come back alive, which would save a lot of trouble; or else, after a lot of discussion, they would be told to go and find beautiful Princesses for themselves, and the one which brought back the most beautiful Princess—but very often that would lead to another discussion. The best way of all was to call in a Fairy to help. A Fairy has all sorts of tricks for finding out about you, and her favourite plan is to pretend to be something else and see what you do.

So the King called in a Fairy and said, 'To-morrow I am sending out my three sons into the world to seek their fortune. I want you to test them for me and find out which is the most fitted to succeed to my throne. If it *should* happen to be Prince Goldenlocks—but, of course, I don't want to influence you in any way.'

'Leave it to me,' said the Fairy. 'You agree, no doubt, that the quality most desirable in a king is love and kindliness—'

'Y-yes,' said the King doubtfully.

'I was sure of it. Well, I have a way of putting this quality to the test which has never yet failed.' And with that she vanished. She could have gone out at the door quite easily, but she preferred to vanish.

I expect you know what her way was. You have read about it often in your fairy books. On the next day, as Prince Proper was coming along the road, she appeared suddenly in front of him in the shape of a poor old woman.

'Please give me something to buy a crust of bread, pretty gentleman,' she pleaded. 'I'm starving.'

Prince Proper looked at her sternly.

'Economically,' he said, 'it is to the advantage of the State that the submerged classes should be a charge on the State itself and not on individuals. The civic interests of the community demand that promiscuous charity should be sternly discouraged. Surely you see that for yourself?'

The Fairy didn't quite. The language had taken her by surprise. In all her previous adventures of this kind, two of the young Princes had refused her roughly, and the third had shared his last piece of bread with her. This adventure was going all wrong.

'Let me explain it to you more fully,' went on Proper, and for an hour and twenty-seven minutes he did so. Then he went on his way, leaving a dazed Fairy behind him.

By and by Prince Clever came along. Suddenly he saw a poor old woman in front of him.

'Please give me something to buy a crust of bread,' she pleaded. 'I'm starving.'

Prince Clever burst into a roar of laughter.

'You don't catch me,' he said. 'I've read about this a hundred times. You're not an old woman at all; you're a Fairy.'

'W-what do you mean?' she stammered.

'This is a silly test of Father's. Well, you can tell him he's got one son who's clever enough to see through him.' And he went on his way.

By and by Prince Goldenlocks came along. I need not say that he did all that you would expect of a third and youngest son who had pink cheeks, long golden hair, and (as I ought to have said before) a very loving nature. He shared his last piece of bread with the poor old woman...

(Surely he will get the throne!)

But the Fairy was an honest Fairy. She did understand Proper's point of view; she had to admit that, if Clever saw through her deception, it was honourable of him to have said so. And though, of course, her loving heart was all for Prince Goldenlocks, she felt that it would not be fair to award the throne to him without a further trial. So she did another thing that she was very fond of doing. She changed herself into a pretty little dove and—right in front of Prince Proper—she flew with a hawk in pursuit of her. '*Now* we shall see,' she said to herself, 'which of the three youths has the softest heart.'

You can guess what Proper said.

'Life,' he said, 'is one constant battle. Nature,' he said, 'is ruthless, and the weakest must go to the wall. If I kill the hawk,' he said, 'I am kind to the dove, but am I,' he said, and I think there was a good deal in this—'am I kind to the caterpillar or whatever it is that the dove eats?' Of course, you know, there *is* that to be thought of. Anyhow, after soliloquizing for forty-seven minutes Prince Proper went on his way; and by and by Prince Clever came along.

You can guess what Clever said.

'My whiskers!' he said, 'this is older than the last. I knew this in my cradle.' With one of those nasty sarcastic laughs that I hate so much he went on his way; and by and by Prince Goldenlocks came along.

(Now then, Goldenlocks, the throne is almost yours!)

You can guess what Goldenlocks said.

'Poor little dove,' he said. 'But I can save its life.'

Rapidly he fitted an arrow to his bow and with careful aim let fly at the pursuing hawk...

I say again that Prince Goldenlocks was the most beautiful youth you have ever seen in your life, and he had a very loving nature. But he was a poor shot.

He hit the dove...

'Is that all?' said Margery.

'That's all,' I said. 'Good night.'

2

THE SAME OLD STORY

We stood in a circle round the parrot's cage and gazed with interest at its occupant. She (Evangeline) was balancing easily on one leg, while with the other leg and her beak she tried to peel a monkey-nut. There are some of us who hate to be watched at meals, particularly when dealing with the dessert, but Evangeline is not of our number.

'There,' said Mrs. Atherley, 'isn't she a beauty?'

I felt that, as the last to be introduced, I ought to say something.

'What do you say to a parrot?' I whispered to Miss Atherley.

'Have a banana,' suggested Reggie.

'I believe you say, "Scratch-a-poll,"' said Miss Atherley, 'but I don't know why.'

'Isn't that rather dangerous? Suppose it retorted "Scratch your own," I shouldn't know a bit how to go on.'

'It can't talk,' said Reggie. 'It's quite a baby—only seven months old. But it's no good showing it your watch; you must think of some other way of amusing it.'

'Break it to me, Reggie. Have I been asked down solely to amuse the parrot, or did any of you others want to see me?'

'Only the parrot,' said Reggie.

Evangeline paid no attention to us. She continued to

wrestle with the monkey-nut. I should say that she was a bird not easily amused.

'Can't it really talk at all?' I asked Mrs. Atherley.

'Not yet. You see, she's only just come over from South America, and isn't used to the climate yet.'

'But that's just the person you'd expect to talk a lot about the weather. I believe you've been had. Write a little note to the poulterers and ask if you can change it. You've got a bad one by mistake.'

'We got it as a bird,' said Mrs. Atherley with dignity, 'not as a gramophone.'

The next morning Evangeline was as silent as ever. Miss Atherley and I surveyed it after breakfast. It was still grappling with a monkey-nut, but no doubt a different one.

'Isn't it *ever* going to talk?' I asked. 'Really, I thought parrots were continually chatting.'

'Yes, but they have to be taught—just like you teach a baby.'

'Are you sure? I quite see that you have to teach them any special things you want them to say, but I thought they were all born with a few simple obvious remarks, like "Poor Polly," or—or "Dash Lloyd George."'

'I don't think so,' said Miss Atherley. 'Not the green ones.'

At dinner that evening, Mr. Atherley being now with us, the question of Evangeline's education was seriously considered.

'The only proper method,' began Mr. Atherley—'By the way,' he said, turning to me, 'you don't know anything about parrots, do you?'

'No,' I said. 'You can go on quite safely.'

'The only proper method of teaching a parrot—I got this from a man in the City this morning—is to give her a word at a time, and to go on repeating it over and over again until she's got hold of it.'

'And after that the parrot goes on repeating it over and over again until you've got sick of it,' said Reggie.

'Then we shall have to be very careful what word we choose,' said Mrs. Atherley.

'What is your favourite word?'

'Well, really—'

'Animal, vegetable, or mineral?' asked Archie.

'This is quite impossible. Every word by itself seems so silly.'

'Not "home" and "mother,"' I said reproachfully.

'You shall recite your little piece in the drawing-room afterwards,' said Miss Atherley to me. 'Think of something sensible now.'

'Yes,' said Mrs. Atherley. 'What's the latest word from London?'

'Kikuyu.'

'What?'

'I can't say it again,' I protested.

'If you can't even say it twice, it's no good for Evangeline.'

A thoughtful silence fell upon us.

'Have you fixed on a name for her yet?' Miss Atherley asked her mother.

'Evangeline, of course.'

'No, I mean a name for her to call *you*. Because if she's going to call you "Auntie" or "Darling," or whatever you decide on, you'd better start by teaching her that.'

And then I had a brilliant idea.

'I've got the very word,' I said. 'It's "hallo." You see, it's a pleasant form of greeting to any stranger, and it will go perfectly with the next word that she's taught, whatever it may be.'

'Supposing it's "wardrobe,"' suggested Reggie, 'or "sardine"?'

'Why not? "Hallo, Sardine" is the perfect title for a *revue*. Witty, subtle, neat—probably the great brain of the Revue King has already evolved it, and is planning the opening scene.'

'Yes, "hallo" isn't at all bad,' said Mr. Atherley. 'Anyway, it's better than "Poor Polly," which is simply morbid. Let's fix on "hallo."'

'Good,' said Mrs. Atherley.

Evangeline said nothing, being asleep under her blanket.

◆

I was down first next morning, having forgotten to wind up my watch overnight. Longing for company, I took the blanket off Evangeline's cage and introduced her to the world again. She stirred sleepily, opened her eyes and blinked at me.

'Hallo, Evangeline,' I said.

She made no reply.

Suddenly a splendid scheme occurred to me. I would teach Evangeline her word now. How it would surprise the others when they came down and said 'Hallo' to her, to find themselves promptly answered back!

'Evangeline,' I said, 'listen. Hallo, hallo, hallo, hallo.' I stopped a moment and went on more slowly. 'Hallo—hallo—hallo.'

It was dull work.

'Hallo,' I said, 'hallo—hallo—hallo,' and then very distinctly, 'Hal-*lo*.'

Evangeline looked at me with an utterly bored face.

'Hallo,' I said, 'hallo—hallo.'

She picked up a monkey-nut and ate it languidly.

'Hallo,' I went on, 'hallo, hallo...hallo, *hallo*, HALLO, HALLO...hallo, hallo—'

She dropped her nut and roused herself for a moment.

'Number engaged,' she snapped, and took another nut.

You needn't believe this. The others didn't when I told them.

3

THE FIRST OF SPRING

There may be gardeners who can appear to be busy all the year round—doing even in the winter, their little bit under glass. But for myself I wait reverently until the 22nd of March is here. Then, Spring having officially arrived, I step out on to the lawn and summon my head-gardener.

'James,' I say, 'the winter is over at last. What have we got in that big brown-looking bed in the middle there?'

'Well, Sir,' he says, 'we don't seem to have anything do we, like?'

'Perhaps there's something down below that hasn't pushed through yet?'

'Maybe there is.'

'I wish you knew more about it,' I say angrily; 'I want to bed out the macaroni there. Have we got a spare bed, with nothing going on underneath?'

'I don't know, Sir. Shall I dig 'em up and have a look?'

'Yes, perhaps you'd better,' I say.

Between ourselves, James is a man of no initiative. He has to be told everything.

However mention of him brings me to my first rule for young gardeners—

'*Never sow Spring Onions and New Potatoes in the same bed.*'

I did this by accident last year. The fact is, when the onions were given to me, I quite thought they were young daffodils; a mistake any one might make. Of course I don't generally keep daffodils and potatoes together; but James swore that the hard round things were tulip bulbs. It is perfectly useless to pay your head-gardener half-a-crown a week if he doesn't know the difference between potatoes and tulip bulbs. Well, anyhow, there they were, in the Herbaceous Border together, and they grew up side by side; the onions getting stronger every day, and the potatoes more sensitive. At last, just when they were ripe for picking, I found that the young onions had actually brought tears to the eyes of the potatoes—to such an extent that the latter were too damp for baking or roasting, and had to be mashed. Now, as everybody knows, mashed potatoes are beastly.

◆

The rhubarb border gives me more trouble than all the rest of the garden. I started it a year ago with the idea of keeping the sun off the young carnations. It acted excellently, and the complexion of the flowers improved tenfold. Then one day I discovered James busily engaged in pulling up the rhubarb.

'What are you doing?' I cried. 'Do you want the young carnations to go all brown?'

'I was going to send some in to the cook,' he grumbled.

'To the cook! What do you mean? Rhubarb isn't a vegetable.'

'No, it's a fruit.'

I looked at James anxiously. He had a large hat on, and the sun couldn't have got to the back of his neck.

'My dear James,' I said, 'I don't pay you half-a-crown a week for being funny. Perhaps we had better make it two shillings in future.'

However, he persisted in his theory that in the spring

people stewed rhubarb in tarts, and ate it!

Well, I have discovered since that this is actually so. People really do grow it in their gardens, not with the idea of keeping the sun off the young carnations, but under the impression that it is a fruit. Consequently I have found it necessary to adopt a firm line with my friends' rhubarb. On arriving at any house for a visit, the first thing I say to my host is, 'May I see your rhubarb bed? I have heard such a lot about it.'

'By all means,' he says, feeling rather flattered, and leads the way into the garden.

'What a glorious sunset,' I say, pointing to the west.

'Isn't it?' he says, turning round; and then I surreptitiously drop a pint of weed-killer on the bed.

Next morning I get up early and paint the roots of the survivors with iodine.

Once my host, who for some reason had got up early too, discovered me.

'What are you doing?' he asked.

'Just painting the roots with iodine,' I said, 'to prevent the rhubarb falling out.'

'To prevent what?'

'To keep the green fly away,' I corrected myself. 'It's the new French intensive system.'

But he was suspicious, and I had to leave two or three stalks untreated. We had those for lunch that day. There was only one thing for a self-respecting man to do. I obtained a large plateful of the weed and emptied the sugar basin and cream jug over it. Then I took a mouthful of the pastry, gave a little start, and said, 'Oh, is this rhubarb? I'm sorry, I didn't know.' Whereupon I pushed my plate away and started on the cheese.

◆

Asparagus: Asparagus wants watching very carefully. It requires to be tended like a child. Frequently I wake up in the middle of the night and wonder if James has remembered to put the hot-water bottle in the asparagus bed. Whenever I get up to look I find that he has forgotten.

He tells me to-day that he is beginning to think that the things which are coming up now are not asparagus after all, but young hyacinths. This is very annoying. I am inclined to fancy that James is not the man he was. For the sake of his reputation in the past I hope he is not.

◆

Potting out: I have spent a very busy morning potting out the nasturtiums. We have them in three qualities, mild, medium, and full. Nasturtiums are extremely peppery flowers, and take offence so quickly that the utmost tact is required to pot them successfully. In a general way all the red or reddish flowers should be potted as soon as they are old enough to stand it, but it is considered bad form among horticulturists to pot the white.

James has been sowing the roses. I wanted all the pink ones in one bed, and all the yellow ones in another, and so on; but James says you never can tell for certain what colour a flower is going to be until it comes up. Of course, any fool could tell then.

'You should go by the picture on the outside of the packet,' I said.

'They're very misleading,' said James.

'Anyhow, they must be all brothers in the same packet.'

'You might have a brother with red hair,' says James.

I hadn't thought of that.

◆

Grafting: Grafting is when you try short approaches over the pergola in somebody else's garden, and break the best tulip. You mend it with a ha'penny stamp and hope that nobody will notice; at any rate not until you have gone away on the Monday. Of course in your own garden you never want to graft.

I hope, at some future time to be allowed—even encouraged—to refer to such things as The Most Artistic Way to Frame Cucumbers, How to Stop Tomatoes Blushing (the homoeopathic method of putting them next to the French beans is now discredited), and Spring Fashions in Fox Gloves. But for the moment I have said enough. The great thing to remember in gardening is that flowers, fruits and vegetables alike can only be cultivated with sympathy. Special attention should be given to backward and delicate plants. They should be encouraged to make the most of themselves. Never forget that flowers, like ourselves, are particular about the company they keep. If a hyacinth droops in the celery bed, put it among the pansies.

But above all, mind, a firm hand with the rhubarb.

4

AFTERNOON SLEEP

'In the afternoon they came unto a land
In which it seemed always afternoon.'

I am like Napoleon in that I can go to sleep at any moment; I am unlike him (I believe) in that I am always doing so. One makes no apology for doing so on Sunday afternoon; the apology indeed should come from the others, the wakeful parties...

'Uncle!'

'Margery.'

'Will you come and play wiv me?'

'I'm rather busy just now,' I said with closed eyes. 'After tea.'

'Why are you raver busy just now? My baby's only raver busy sometimes.'

'Well then, you know what it's like; how important it is that one shouldn't be disturbed.'

'But you must be beturbed when I ask you to come and play wiv me.'

'Oh, well...what shall we play at?'

'Trains,' said Margery eagerly.

When we play at trains I have to be a tunnel. I don't know

if you have ever been a tunnel? No; well, it's an over-rated profession.

'We won't play trains,' I announced firmly, 'because it's Sunday.'

'Why not because it's Sunday?'

(Oh, you little pagan!)

'Hasn't Mummy told you about Sunday?'

'Oh, yes, Maud did tell me,' said Margery casually. Then she gave an innocent little smile. 'Oh, I called Mummy Maud,' she said in pretended surprise. 'I quite fought. I was upstairs!'

I hope you follow. The manners and customs of good society must be observed on the ground floor where visitors may happen; upstairs one relaxes a little.

'Do you know,' Margery went on with the air of a discoverer, 'you mustn't say "prayers" downstairs. Or "corsets."'

'I never do,' I affirmed. 'Well, anyhow I never will again.'

'Why mayn't you?'

'I don't know,' I said sleepily.

'Say prehaps.'

'Well—prehaps it's because your mother tells you not to.'

'Well, 'at's a silly fing to say,' said Margery scornfully.

'It is. I'm thoroughly ashamed of it. I apologise. Good night.' And I closed my eyes again...

'I fought you were going to play wiv me, Mr. Bingle,' sighed Margery to herself.

'My name is not Bingle,' I said, opening one eye.

'Why isn't it Bingle?'

'The story is a very long and sad one. When I wake up I will tell it to you. Good night.'

'Tell it to me now.'

There was no help for it.

'Once upon a time,' I said rapidly, 'there was a man called Bingle, Oliver Bingle, and he married a lady called Pringle. And his brother married a lady called Jingle; and his other brother married a Miss Wingle. And his cousin remained single... That is all.'

'Oh, I see,' said Margery doubtfully. 'Now will you play wiv me?'

How can one resist the pleading of a young child?

'All right,' I said. 'We'll pretend I'm a little girl, and you're my mummy, and you've just put me to bed... Good night, mummy dear.'

'Oh, but I must cover you up.' She fetched a table-cloth, and a pram-cover, and *The Times*, and a handkerchief, and the cat, and a doll's what-I-mustn't-say-downstairs, and a cushion; and she covered me up and tucked me in. ''Ere, 'ere, now go to sleep, my darling,' she said, and kissed me lovingly.

'Oh, Margie, you dear,' I whispered.

'You called me "Margie"!' she cried in horror.

'I meant "Mummy." Good night.'

One, two, three seconds passed rapidly.

'It's morning,' said a bright voice in my ear. 'Get up.'

'I'm very ill,' I pleaded; 'I want to stay in bed all day.'

'But your dear uncle,' said Margery, inventing hastily, 'came last night after you were in bed, and stayed 'e night. Do you see? And he wants you to sit on him in bed and talk to him.'

'Where is he? Show me the bounder.'

''Ere he is,' said Margery, pointing at me.

'But look here, I can't sit on my own chest and talk to myself. I'll take the two parts if you insist, Sir Herbert, but I can't play them simultaneously. Not even Irving—'

'Why can't you play them simrulaleously?'

'Well, I can't. Margie, will you let me go to sleep?'

'Nope,' said Margery, shaking her head.

'You should say, "No thank you, revered and highly respected Uncle."'

'No *hank* you, Mr. Cann.'

'I have already informed you that my name is not Bingle and I have now to add that neither is it Cann.'

'Why neiver is it Cann?'

'That isn't grammar. You should say, "Why can it not either?"'

'Why?'

'I don't know.'

'Say prehaps.'

'No, I can't even say prehaps.'

'Well, say I shall understand when I'm a big girl.'

'You'll understand when you're a big girl, Margery,' I said solemnly.

'Oh, I see.'

'That's right. Now then, what about going to sleep?'

She was silent for a moment, and I thought I was safe. Then.

'Uncle, just tell me—why was 'at little boy crying vis morning?'

'Which little boy?'

'Ve one in 'e road.'

'Oh, that one. Well, he was crying because his Uncle hadn't had any sleep all night, and when he tried to go to sleep in the afternoon—'

'Say prehaps again.'

My first rejected contribution! I sighed and had another shot. 'Well, then,' I said gallantly, 'it must have been because he hadn't got a sweet little girl of three to play with him.'

'Yes,' said Margery, nodding her head thoughtfully, ''at was it.'

5

WRONGLY ATTRIBUTED

You've heard of Willy Ferrero, the Boy Conductor? A musical prodigy, seven years old, who will order the fifth oboe out of the Albert Hall as soon as look at him. Well, he has a rival.

Willy, as perhaps you know, does not play any instrument himself; he only conducts. His rival (Johnny, as I think of him) does not conduct as yet; at least, not audibly. His line is the actual manipulation of the pianoforte—the Paderewski touch. Johnny lives in the flat below, and I hear him touching.

On certain mornings in the week—no need to specify them—I enter my library and give myself up to literary composition. On the same mornings little Johnny enters his music-room (underneath) and gives himself up to musical composition. Thus we are at work together.

The worst of literary composition is this: that when you have got hold of what you feel is a really powerful idea, you find suddenly that you have been forestalled by some earlier writer—Sophocles or Shakespeare or George R. Sims. Then you have to think again. This frequently happens to me upstairs; and downstairs poor Johnny will find to his horror one day that his great work has already been given to the world by another—a certain Dr. John Bull.

Johnny, in fact, is discovering 'God Save the King' with one finger.

As I dip my pen in the ink and begin to write, Johnny strikes up. On the first day when this happened, some three months ago, I rose from my chair and stood stiffly through the performance—an affair of some minutes, owing to a little difficulty with 'Send him victorious,' a line which always bothers Johnny. However, he got right through it at last, after harking back no more than twice, and I sat down to my work again. Generally speaking, 'God Save the King' ends a show; it would be disloyal to play any other tune after that. Johnny quite saw this...and so began to play 'God Save the King' again.

I hope that His Majesty, the Lord Chamberlain, the late Dr. Bull, or whoever is most concerned, will sympathize with me when I say that this time I remained seated. I have my living to earn.

From that day Johnny has interpreted Dr. John Bull's favourite composition nine times every morning. As this has been going on for three months, and as the line I mentioned has two special rehearsals to itself before coming out right, you can easily work out how many send-him-victoriouses Johnny and I have collaborated in. About two thousand.

Very well. Now, you ask yourself, why did I not send a polite note to Johnny's father asking him to restrain his little boy from over-composition, begging him not to force the child's musical genius too quickly, imploring him (in short) to lock up the piano and lose the key? What kept me from this course? The answer is 'Patriotism.' Those deep feelings for his country which one man will express glibly by rising nine times during the morning at the sound of the National Anthem, another will direct to more solid uses. It was my duty, I felt, not to discourage Johnny. He was showing qualities which could not fail, when he grew up, to be of value to the nation. Loyalty, musical genius, determination, patience, industry—never before have these qualities been so finely united in a child of six. Was I to say a single word to disturb the delicate balance of such a boy's mind? At six one is extraordinarily susceptible to outside influence. A word from his father to the effect that the gentleman above was getting sick of it, and Johnny's whole life might be altered.

No, I would bear it grimly.

And then, yesterday, who should write to me but Johnny's father himself. This was the letter:

'Dear Sir—I do not wish to interfere unduly in the affairs of the other occupants of these flats, but I feel bound to call your attention to the fact that for many weeks now there has been a flow of water from your bathroom, which has penetrated through the ceiling of my bathroom, particularly after you have been using the room in the mornings. May I therefore beg you to be more careful in future not to splash or spill water on your floor, seeing that it causes inconvenience to the tenants beneath you?

'Yours faithfully, Jno. McAndrew.'

You can understand how I felt about this. For months I had been suffering Johnny in silence; yet, at the first little drop of water from above, Johnny's father must break out into violent abuse of me. A fine reward! Well, Johnny's future could look after itself now; anyhow, he was doomed with a selfish father like that.

'Dear Sir,' I answered defiantly, 'Now that we are writing to each other I wish to call your attention to the fact that for many months past there has been a constant flow of one-fingered music from your little boy, which penetrates through the floor of my library and makes all work impossible. May I beg you, therefore, to see that your child is taught a new tune immediately, seeing that the National Anthem has lost its first freshness for the tenants above him?'

His reply to this came to-day.

'Dear Sir,—I have no child.

'Yours faithfully, Jno. McAndrew.'

I was so staggered that I could only think of one adequate retort.

'DEAR SIR,' I wrote,—'I never have a bath.'

◆

So that's the end of Johnny, my boy prodigy, for whom I have suffered so long. It is not Johnny but Jno. who struggles with the National Anthem. He will give up music now, for he knows I have the bulge on him; I can flood his bathroom whenever I like. Probably he will learn something quieter—like painting. Anyway, Dr. John Bull's masterpiece will rise no more through the ceiling of the flat below.

On referring to my encyclopedia, I see that, according to some authorities, 'God Save the King' is 'wrongly attributed' to Dr. Bull. Well, I wrongly attributed it to Johnny. It is easy to make these mistakes.

6

THE BIRTHDAY PRESENT

'It's my birthday to-morrow,' said Mrs. Jeremy as she turned the pages of her engagement book.

'Bless us, so it is,' said Jeremy. 'You're thirty-nine or twenty-seven or something. I must go and examine the wine-cellar. I believe there's one bottle left in the Apollinaris bin. It's the only stuff in the house that fizzes.'

'Jeremy! I'm only twenty-six.'

'You don't look it, darling; I mean you do look it, dear. What I mean—well, never mind that. Let's talk about birthday presents. Think of something absolutely tremendous for me to give you.'

'A rope of pearls.'

'I didn't mean that sort of tremendousness,' said Jeremy quickly. 'Anyone could give you a rope of pearls; it's simply a question of overdrawing enough from the bank. I meant something difficult that would really prove my love for you— like Lloyd George's ear or the Kaiser's cigar-holder. Something where I could kill somebody for you first. I am in a very devoted mood this morning.'

'Are you really?' smiled Mrs. Jeremy. 'Because—'

'I am. So is Baby, unfortunately. She will probably want to give you something horribly expensive. Between ourselves, dear, I shall be glad when Baby is old enough to buy her own presents for her mamma. Last Christmas her idea of a complete edition of Meredith and a pair of silver-backed brushes nearly ruined me.'

'You won't be ruined this time, Jeremy. I don't want you to give me anything; I want you to show that devotion of yours by doing something for me.'

'Anything,' said Jeremy grandly. 'Shall I swim the Channel? I was practising my new trudgeon stroke in the bath this morning.' He got up from his chair and prepared to give an exhibition of it.

'No, nothing like that.' Mrs. Jeremy hesitated, looked anxiously at him, and then went boldly at it. 'I want you to go in for that physical culture that everyone's talking about.'

'Who's everyone? Cook hasn't said a word to me on the subject; neither has Baby; neither has—'

'Mrs. Hodgkin was talking to me about it yesterday. She was saying how thin you were looking.'

'The scandal that goes on in these villages,' sighed Jeremy. 'And the Vicar's wife too. Dear, all this is weeks and weeks old; I suppose it has only just reached the Vicarage. Do let us be up-to-date. Physical culture has been quite *demode* since last Thursday.'

'Well, *I* never saw anything in the paper—'

'Knowing what wives are, I hid it from you. Let us now, my dear wife, talk of something else.'

'Jeremy! Not for my birthday present?' said his wife in a reproachful voice. 'The Vicar does them every morning,' she added casually.

'Poor beggar! But it's what Vicars are for.' Jeremy chuckled to himself. 'I should love to see him,' he said. 'I suppose it's private, though. Perhaps if I said "Press"—'

'You are thin, you know.'

'My dear, the proper way to get fat is not to take violent exercise, but to lie in a hammock all day and drink milk. Besides, do you want a fat husband? Does Baby want a fat father? You wouldn't like, at your next garden party, to have everybody asking you in a whisper, "Who is the enormously stout gentleman?" If Nature made me thin—or, to be more accurate, slender and of a pleasing litheness—let us believe that she knew best.'

'It isn't only thinness; these exercises keep you young and well and active in mind.'

'Like the Vicar?'

'He's only just begun,' said his wife hastily.

'Let's wait a bit and watch him,' suggested Jeremy. 'If his sermons really get better, then I'll think about it seriously. I make you a present of his baldness; I shan't ask for any improvement there.'

Mrs. Jeremy went over to her husband and patted the top of his head.

'"In a very devoted mood this morning,"' she quoted.

Jeremy looked unhappy.

'What pains me most about this,' he said, 'is the revelation of your shortcomings as a wife. You ought to think me the picture of manly beauty. Baby does. She thinks that, next to the postman, I am one of the—'

'So you are, dear.'

'Well, why not leave it? Really, I can't waste my time fattening refined gold and stoutening the lily. I am a busy man. I walk up and down the pergola, I keep a dog, I paint little water-colours, I am treasurer of the cricket club; my life is full of activities.'

'This only takes a quarter of an hour before your bath, Jeremy.'

'I am shaving then; I should cut myself and get all the soap in my eyes. It would be most dangerous. When you were a widow, and Baby and the pony were orphans, you and Mrs. Hodgkin would be sorry. But it would be too late. The Vicar, tearing himself away from Position 5 to conduct the funeral service—'

'Jeremy, *don't!*'

'Ah, woman, now I move you. You are beginning to see what you were in danger of doing. Death I laugh at; but a fat death— the death of a stout man who has swallowed the shaving-brush through taking too deep a breath before beginning Exercise 3, that is more than I can bear.'

'Jeremy!'

'When I said I wanted to kill someone for you, I didn't think you would suggest myself, least of all that you wanted me fattened up like a Christmas turkey first. To go down to posterity as the large-bodied gentleman who inhaled the badger's hair; to be billed in the London press in the words, "Curious Fatal Accident to Adipose Treasurer"—to do this simply by way of celebrating your twenty-sixth birthday, when we actually have a bottle of Apollinaris left in the Apollinaris bin—darling, you cannot have been thinking—'

His wife patted his head again gently. 'Oh, Jeremy, you hopeless person,' she sighed. 'Give me a new sunshade. I want one badly.'

'No,' said Jeremy, 'Baby shall give you that. For myself I am still feeling that I should like to kill somebody for you. Lloyd George? No. F.E. Smith? N-no...' He rubbed his head thoughtfully. 'Who invented those exercises?' he asked suddenly.

'A German, I think.'

'Then,' said Jeremy, buttoning up his coat, 'I shall go and kill him.'

7

A CROWN OF SORROWS

There is something on my mind, of which I must relieve myself. If I am ever to face the world again with a smile I must share my trouble with others. I cannot bear my burden alone.

Friends, I have lost my hat. Will the gentleman who took it by mistake, and forgot to leave his own in its place, kindly return my hat to me at once?

I am very miserable without my hat. It was one of those nice soft ones with a dent down the middle to collect the rain; one of those soft hats which wrap themselves so lovingly round the cranium that they ultimately absorb the personality of the wearer underneath, responding to his every emotion. When people said nice things about me my hat would swell in sympathy; when they said nasty things, or when I had had my hair cut, it would adapt itself automatically to my lesser requirements. In a word, it fitted—and that is more than can be said for your hard unyielding bowler.

My hat and I dropped into a hall of music one night last week. I placed it under the seat, put a coat on it to keep it warm, and settled down to enjoy myself. My hat could see nothing, but it knew that it would hear all about the entertainment on the way home. When the last moving picture had moved away, my hat and I prepared to depart together. I drew out the coat and felt around for my—Where on earth...

I was calm at first.

'Excuse me,' I said politely to the man next to me, 'but have you got two hats?'

'Several,' he replied, mistaking my meaning.

I dived under the seat again, and came up with some more dust.

'Someone,' I said to a programme girl, 'has taken my hat.'

'Have you looked under the seat for it?' she asked.

It was such a sound suggestion that I went under the seat for the third time.

'It may have been kicked further along,' suggested another attendant. She walked up and down the row looking for it, and, in case somebody had kicked it into the row above, walked up and down that one too; and, in case somebody had found touch with it on the other side of the house, many other girls spread themselves in pursuit; and soon we had the whole pack hunting for it.

Then the fireman came up, suspecting the worst. I told him it was even worse than that—my hat had been stolen.

He had a flash of inspiration.

'Are you sure you brought it with you?' he asked.

The programme girls seemed to think that it would solve the whole mystery if I hadn't brought it with me.

'Are you sure you are the fireman?' I said coldly.

He thought for a moment, and then unburdened himself of another idea.

'Perhaps it's just been kicked under the seat,' he said.

I left him under the seat and went downstairs with a heavy heart. At the door I said to the hall porter, 'Have you seen anybody going out with two hats by mistake?'

'What's the matter?' he said. 'Lost your hat?'

'It has been stolen.'

'Have you looked under the seats? It may have been kicked along a bit.'

'Perhaps I'd better see the manager,' I said. 'Is it any good looking under the seats for HIM?'

'I expect it's just been kicked along a bit,' the hall porter repeated confidently. 'I'll come up with you and look for it.'

'If there's any more talk about being kicked along a bit,' I said bitterly, 'somebody WILL be. I want the manager.'

I was led to the manager's room, and there I explained the matter to him. He was very pleasant about it.

'I expect you haven't looked for it properly,' he said, with a charming smile. 'Just take this gentleman up,' he added to the hall porter, 'and find his hat for him. It has probably been kicked under one of the other seats.'

We were smiled irresistibly out, and I was dragged up to the grand circle again. The seats by this time were laid out in white draperies; the house looked very desolate; I knew that my poor hat was dead. With an air of cheery confidence the hall porter turned into the first row of seats...

'It may have been kicked on to the stage,' I said, as he began to slow down. 'It may have jumped into one of the boxes. It may have turned into a rabbit. You know, I expect you aren't looking for it properly.'

The manager was extremely sympathetic when we came back to him. He said, 'Oh, I'm sorry.' Just like that—'Oh, I'm sorry.'

'My hat,' I said firmly, 'has been stolen.'

'I'm sorry,' he repeated with a bored smile, and turned to look at himself in the glass.

Then I became angry with him and his attendants and his whole blessed theatre.

'My hat,' I said bitingly, 'has been stolen from me—while I slept.'

◆

You must have seen me wearing it in the dear old days. Greeny brown it was in colour; but it wasn't the colour that drew your eyes to it—no, nor yet the shape, nor the angle at which it sat. It was just the essential rightness of it. If you have ever seen a hat which you felt instinctively was a clever hat, an alive hat, a profound hat, then that was my hat—and that was myself underneath it.

8

MY SECRETARY

When, five years ago, I used to write long letters to Margery, for some reason or other she never wrote back. To save her face I had to answer the letters myself—a tedious business. Still, I must admit that the warmth and geniality of the replies gave me a certain standing with my friends, who had not looked for me to be so popular. After some months, however, pride stepped in. One cannot pour out letter after letter to a lady without any acknowledgment save from oneself. And when even my own acknowledgments began to lose their first warmth—when, for instance, I answered four pages about my new pianola with the curt reminder that I was learning to walk and couldn't be bothered with music, why, then at last I saw that a correspondence so one-sided would have to come to an end. I wrote a farewell letter and replied to it with tears...

But, bless you, that was nearly five years ago. Each morning now, among the usual pile of notes on my plate from duchesses, publishers, moneylenders, actor-managers and what-not, I find, likely enough, an envelope in Margery's own handwriting.

Not only is my address printed upon it legibly, but there are also such extra directions to the postman as 'England' and 'Important' for its more speedy arrival. And inside—well, I give you the last but seven.

'MY DEAR UNCLE I thot you wher coming to see me tonight but you didnt why didnt you baby has p t o hurt her knee isnt that a pity I have some new toys isnt that jolly we didnt have our five minutes so will you krite to me and tell me all about p t o your work from your loving little MARGIE.'

I always think that footnotes to a letter are a mistake, but there are one or two things I should like to explain.

(a) Just as some journalists feel that without the word 'economic' a leading article lacks tone, so Margery feels, and I agree with her, that a certain *cachet* is lent to a letter by a p. t. o. at the bottom of each page.

(b) There are lots of grown-up people who think that 'write' is spelt 'rite.' Margery knows that this is not so. She knows that there is a silent letter in front of the 'r,' which doesn't do anything, but likes to be there. Obviously, if nobody is going to take any notice of this extra letter, it doesn't much matter what it is. Margery happened to want to make a 'k' just then; at a pinch it could be as silent as a 'w.' You will please, therefore, regard the 'k' in 'Krite' as absolutely noiseless.

(c) Years ago I claimed the privilege to monopolise on the occasional evenings when I was there, Margery's last ten minutes before she goes back to some heaven of her own each night. This privilege was granted; it being felt, no doubt, that she owed me some compensation for my early secretarial work on her behalf. We used to spend the ten minutes in listening to my telling a fairy story, always the same one. One day the authorities stepped in and announced that in future the ten minutes would be reduced to five. The procedure seemed to me absolutely illegal (and I should like to bring an action against somebody) but it certainly did put the lid on my fairy story, of which I was getting more than a little tired.

'Tell me about Beauty and the Beast,' said Margery as usual, that evening.

'There's not time,' I said. 'We've only five minutes to-night.'

'Oh! Then tell me all the work you've done to-day.'

(A little unkind, you'll agree, but you know what relations are.)

And so now I have to cram the record of my day's work into five breathless minutes. You will understand what bare justice I can do it in the time.

I am sorry that these footnotes have grown so big; let us leave them and return to the letter. There are many ways of answering such a letter. One might say, 'MY DEAR MARGERY,— It was jolly to get a real letter from you at last—' but the 'at last' would seem rather tactless considering what had passed years before. Or one might say, 'MY DEAR MARGERY,—Thank you for your jolly letter. I am so sorry about baby's knee and so glad about your toys. Perhaps if you gave one of the toys to baby, then her knee—' But I feel sure that Margery would expect me to do better than that.

In the particular case of this last letter but seven I wrote:

'DEAREST MARGERY,—Thank you for your sweet letter.
I had a very busy day at the office or I would have come
to see you. P.T.O.

[Transcriber's note: Page break in original.]

—I hope to be down next week and then I will tell you
all about my work; but I have a lot more to do now, and
so I must say good-bye. Your loving UNCLE.'

There is perhaps nothing in that which demands an immediate answer, but with business-like promptitude Margery replied:

'MY DEAR UNCLE thank you for your letter I am glad
you are coming next week baby is quite well now are you
p t o coming on Thursday next week or not say yes if you

are I am p t o sorry you are working so hard from your loving MARGIE.'

I said 'Yes,' and that I was her loving uncle. It seemed to be then too late for a 'P.T.O.,' but I got one in and put on the back, 'Love to Baby.' The answer came by return of post:

'MY DEAR UNCLE thank you for your letter come erly on p t o Thursday come at half past nothing baby sends her love and so do p t o I my roking horse has a sirrup broken isnt that a pity say yes or no good-bye from your loving MARGIE.'

Of course I thanked Baby for her love and gave my decision that it *was* a pity about the rocking-horse. I did it in large capitals, which (as I ought to have said before) is the means of communication between Margery and her friends. For some reason or other I find printing capitals to be more tiring than the ordinary method of writing.

'MY DEAR UNCLE,' wrote Margery—

But we need not go into that. What I want to say is this: I love to get letters, particularly these, but I hate writing them, particularly in capitals. Years ago I used to answer Margery's letter for her. It is now her turn to answer mine for me.

9

THE ART OF CONVERSATION

'In conversation,' said somebody (I think it was my grandfather), 'there should always be a give and take. The ball must be kept rolling.' If he had ever had a niece two years old, I don't think he would have bothered.

'What's 'at?' said Margery, pointing suddenly.

'That,' I said, stroking it, 'is dear uncle's nose.'

'What's 'at?'

'Take your finger away. Ah, yes, that is dear uncle's eye. The left one.'

'Dear uncle's left one,' said Margery thoughtfully. 'What's it doing?'

'Thinking.'

'What's finking?'

'What dear uncle does every afternoon after lunch.'

'What's lunch?'

'Eggs, sardines, macaroons—everything.'

With a great effort Margery resisted the temptation to ask what 'everything' was (a difficult question), and made a statement of her own.

'Santa Claus bring Margie a balloon from Daddy,' she announced.

'A balloon! How jolly!' I said with interest. 'What sort are you having? One of those semi-detached ones with the gas laid on, or the pink ones with a velvet collar?'

'Down chimney,' said Margery.

'Oh, that kind. Do you think—I mean, isn't it rather—'

'Tell Margie a story about a balloon.'

'Bother,' I murmured.

'What's bovver?'

'Bother is what you say when relations ask you to tell them a story about a balloon. It means, "But for the fact that we both have the Montmorency blood in our veins, I should be compelled to decline your kind invitation, all the stories I know about balloons being stiff 'uns." It also means, "Instead of talking about balloons, won't you sing me a little song?"'

'Nope,' said Margery.

'Bother, she's forgotten her music.'

'What did you say, uncle dear; what did you say?'

I sighed and began.

'Once upon a time there was a balloon, a dear little toy balloon, and and—'

'What's 'at?' asked Margery, making a dab at my chest. 'What's 'at, uncle dear?'

'That,' I said, 'is a button. More particularly a red waistcoat button. More particularly still, my top red waistcoat button.'

'What's 'at?' she asked, going down one.

'That is a button. Description: second red waistcoat. Parents living: both. Infectious diseases: scarlet fever slightly once.'

'What's 'at?'

'That's a—ah, yes, a button. The third. A good little chap, but not so chubby as his brothers. He couldn't go down to Margate with them last year, and so, of course—Well, as I was saying, there was once a balloon, and—'

'What's a-a-'at?' said Margery, bending forward suddenly and kissing it.

'Look here, you've jolly well got to enclose a stamped addressed envelope with the next question. As a matter of fact, though you won't believe me, that again is a button.'

'What's 'at?' asked Margery, digging at the fifth button.

'Owing to extreme pressure on space,' I began... 'Thank you. That also is a button. Its responsibility is greater than that of its brethren. The crash may come at any moment. Luckily it has booked its passage to the—where was I? Oh yes—well, this balloon—'

'What's 'at?' said Margery, pointing to the last one.

'I must have written notice of that question. I can't tell you offhand.'

'What's 'at, uncle dear?'

'Well, I don't know, Margie. It looks something like a collar stud, only somehow you wouldn't expect to find a collar stud there. Of course it may have slipped... Or could it be one of those red beads, do you think?... N-no—no, it isn't a bead... And it isn't a raspberry, because this is the wrong week for raspberries. Of course it might be a—By Jove, I've got it! It's a button.'

I gave the sort of war-whoop with which one announces these discoveries, and Margery whooped too.

'A button,' she cried. 'A dear little button!' She thought for a moment. 'What's a button?'

This was ridiculous.

'You don't mean to say,' I reproached her, 'that I've got to tell you now what a button is. That,' I added severely, pointing to the top of my waistcoat, 'is a button.'

'What's 'at?' said Margery, pointing to the next one.

I looked at her in horror. Then I began to talk very quickly. 'There was once a balloon,' I said rapidly, 'a dear little boy balloon—I mean toy balloon, and this balloon was a jolly little balloon just two minutes old, and he wasn't always asking silly questions, and when he fell down and exploded himself they used to wring him out and say, "Come, come now, be a little airship about it," and so—'

'What's 'at?' asked Margery, pointing to the top button.

There was only one way out of it. I began to sing a carol in a very shrill voice.

All the artist rose in Margery.

'Don't sing,' she said hurriedly; 'Margie sing. What shall Margie sing, uncle?'

Before I could suggest anything she was off. It was a scandalous song. She began by announcing that she wanted to be among the boys, and (anticipating my objections) assured me that it was no good kicking up a noise, because it was no fun going out when there weren't any boys about, you were so lonely-onely-onely...

Here the tune became undecided; and, a chance word recalling another context to her mind, she drifted suddenly into a hymn, and sang it with the same religious fervour as she had sung the other, her fair head flung back, and her hazel eyes gazing into Heaven...

I listened carefully. This was a bit I didn't recognise... The tune wavered for a moment...and out of it these words emerged triumphant—

'Talk of me to the boys you meet.

Remember me kindly to Regent Street.

And give them my love in the—'

'What's 'at, uncle?'

'That,' I said, stroking it, 'is dear uncle's nose.'

'What's—'

By the way, would you like it all over again? No? Oh, very well.

10

BACHELOR RELICS

'Do you happen to want,' I said to Henry, 'an opera hat that doesn't op? At least it only works on one side.'

'No,' said Henry.

'To anyone who buys my opera hat for a large sum I am giving away four square yards of linoleum, a revolving bookcase, two curtain rods, a pair of spring-grip dumb-bells, and an extremely patent mouse-trap.'

'No,' said Henry again.

'The mouse-trap,' I pleaded, 'is unused. That is to say, no mouse has used it yet. My mouse-trap has never been blooded.'

'I don't want it myself,' said Henry, 'but I know a man who does.'

'Henry, you know everybody. For Heaven's sake introduce me to your friend. Why does he particularly want a mouse-trap?'

'He doesn't. He wants anything that's old. Old clothes, old carpets, anything that's old he'll buy.'

He seemed to be exactly the man I wanted.

'Introduce me to your fellow clubman,' I said firmly.

That evening I wrote to Henry's friend, Mr. Bennett. 'Dear Sir,' I wrote, 'if you would call upon me to-morrow I should like to show you some really old things, all genuine antiques. In particular I would call your attention to an old opera hat of exquisite workmanship and a mouse-trap of chaste and handsome design. I have also a few yards of Queen Anne linoleum of a circular pattern which I think will please you. My James the First spring-grip dumb-bells and Louis Quatorze curtain-rods are well known to connoisseurs. A genuine old cork bedroom suite, comprising one bath-mat, will also be included in the sale. Yours faithfully.'

On second thoughts I tore the letter up and sent Mr. Bennett a postcard asking him to favour the undersigned with a call at 10.30 prompt. And at 10.30 prompt he came.

I had expected to see a bearded patriarch with a hooked nose and three hats on his head, but Mr. Bennett turned out to be a very spruce gentleman, wearing (I was sorry to see) much better clothes than the opera hat I proposed to sell him. He became businesslike at once.

'Just tell me what you want to sell,' he said, whipping out a pocket-book, 'and I'll make a note of it. I take anything.'

I looked round my spacious apartment and wondered what to begin with.

'The revolving book-case,' I announced.

'I'm afraid there's very little sale for revolving book-cases now,' he said, as he made a note of it.

'As a matter of fact,' I pointed out, 'this one doesn't revolve. It got stuck some years ago.'

He didn't seem to think that this would increase the rush, but he made a note of it.

'Then the writing-desk.'

'The what?'

'The Georgian bureau. A copy of an old twentieth-century escritoire.'

'Walnut?' he said, tapping it.

'Possibly. The value of this Georgian writing-desk, however, lies not in the wood but in the literary associations.'

'Ah! My customers don't bother much about that, but still—whose was it?'

'Mine,' I said with dignity, placing my hand in the breast pocket of my coat. 'I have written many charming things at that desk. My "Ode to a Bell-push," my "Thoughts on Asia," my—'

'Anything else in this room?' said Mr. Bennett. 'Carpet, curtains—'

'Nothing else,' I said coldly.

We went into the bedroom and, gazing on the linoleum, my enthusiasm returned to me.

'The linoleum,' I said, with a wave of the hand.

'Very much worn,' said Mr. Bennett.

I called his attention to the piece under the bed.

'Not under there,' I said. 'I never walk on that piece. It's as good as new.'

He made a note. 'What else?' he said.

I showed him round the collection. He saw the Louis Quatorze curtain-rods, the cork bedroom suite, the Caesarian nail-brush (quite bald), the antique shaving-mirror with genuine crack—he saw it all. And then we went back into the other rooms and found some more things for him.

'Yes,' he said, consulting his note-book. 'And now how would you like me to buy these?'

'At a large price,' I said. 'If you have brought your cheque-book I'll lend you a pen.'

'You want me to make you an offer? Otherwise I should sell them by auction for you, deducting ten per cent commission.'

'Not by auction,' I said impulsively. 'I couldn't bear to know how much, or rather how little, my Georgian bureau fetched. It was there, as I think I told you, that I wrote my *Guide to the Round Pond*. Give me an inclusive price for the lot, and never, never let me know the details.'

He named an inclusive price. It was something under a hundred and fifty pounds. I shouldn't have minded that if it had only been a little over ten pounds. But it wasn't.

'Right,' I agreed. 'And, oh, I was nearly forgetting. There's an old opera hat of exquisite workmanship, which—'

'Ah, now, clothes had much better be sold by auction. Make a pile of all you don't want and I'll send round a sack for them. I have an auction sale every Wednesday.'

'Very well. Send round to-morrow. And you might—er— also send round a—er—cheque for—quite so. Well, then, good morning.'

When he had gone I went into my bedroom and made a pile of my opera hat. It didn't look very impressive—hardly worth having a sack specially sent round for it. To keep it company I collected an assortment of clothes. It pained me to break up my wardrobe in this way, but I wanted the bidding for my opera hat to be brisk, and a few preliminary suits would warm the public up. Altogether it was a goodly pile when it was done. The opera hat perched on the top, half of it only at work.

◆

To-day I received from Mr. Bennett a cheque, a catalogue, and an account. The catalogue was marked 'Lots 172-179.' Somehow I felt that my opera hat would be Lot 176. I turned to it in the account.

'*Lot 176*—Six shillings.'

'It did well,' I said. 'Perhaps in my heart of hearts I hoped for seven and sixpence, but six shillings—yes, it was a good hat.'

And then I turned to the catalogue.

'Lot 176—Frock-coat and vest, dress-coat and vest, ditto, pair of trousers and opera hat.'

'And opera hat.' Well, well. At least it had the position of honour at the end. My opera hat was starred.

11

A CHAPTER OF ACCIDENTS

John walked eight miles over the cliffs to the nearest town in order to buy tobacco. He came back to the farmhouse with no tobacco and the news that he had met some friends in the town who had invited us to dinner and Bridge the next evening.

'But that's no reason why you should have forgotten the tobacco,' I said.

'One can't remember everything. I accepted for both of us. We needn't dress. Put on that nice blue flannel suit of yours—'

'And that nice pair of climbing boots with the nails.'

'Is that all you've got?'

'All I'm going to walk eight miles in on a muddy path.'

'Then we shall have to take a bag with us. And we can put in pyjamas and stay the night at an hotel; it will save us walking back in the dark. We don't want to lose you over the cliff.'

I took out a cigar.

'This is the last,' I said. 'If, instead of wandering about and collecting invitations, you had only remembered—Shall we cut it up or smoke half each?'

'Call,' said John, bringing out a penny. 'Heads it is. You begin.'

I struck a match and began.

Next day, after lunch, John brought out his little brown bag. 'It won't be very heavy,' he said, 'and we can carry it in turns. An hour each.'

'I don't think that's quite fair,' I said. 'After all, it's YOUR bag. If you take it for an hour and a half, I don't mind taking the other half.'

'Your shoes are heavier than mine, anyhow.'

'My pyjamas weigh less. Such a light blue as they are.'

'Ah, but my tooth-brush has lost seven bristles. That makes a difference.'

'What I say is, let every man carry his own bag. This is a rotten business, John. I don't wish to be anything but polite, but for a silly ass commend me to the owner of that brown thing.'

John took no notice and went on packing.

'I shall buy a collar in the town,' he said.

'Better let me do it for you. You would only go getting an invitation to a garden-party from the haberdasher. And that would mean another eight miles with a portmanteau.'

'There we are,' said John, as he closed the bag, 'quite small and light. Now, who'll take the first hour?'

'We'd better toss, if you're quite sure you won't carry it all the way. Tails. Just my luck.'

John looked out of the window and then at his watch.

'They say two to three is the hottest hour of the day,' he said. 'It will be cooler later on. I shall put you in.'

I led the way up the cliffs with that wretched bag. I insisted upon that condition anyhow—that the man with the bag should lead the way. I wasn't going to have John dashing off at six miles an hour, and leaving himself only two miles at the end.

'But you can come and talk to me,' I said to him after ten minutes of it. 'I only meant that I was going to set the pace.'

'No, no, I like watching you. You do it so gracefully. This is my man,' he explained to some children who were blackberrying. 'He is just carrying my bag over the cliffs for me. No, he is not very strong.'

'You wait,' I growled.

John laughed. 'Fifty minutes more,' he said. And then after a little silence, 'I think the bag-carrying profession is overrated. What made you take it up, my lad? The drink? Ah, just so. Dear, dear, what a lesson to all of us.'

'There's a good time coming,' I murmured to myself, and changed hands for the eighth time.

'I don't care what people say,' said John, argumentatively; 'brown and blue DO go together. If you wouldn't mind—'

For the tenth time I rammed the sharp corner of the bag into the back of my knee.

'There, that's what I mean. You see it perfectly like that—the brown against the blue of the flannel. Thank you very much.'

I stumbled up a steep little bit of slippery grass, and told myself that in three-quarters of an hour I would get some of my own back again. He little knew how heavy that bag could become.

'They say,' said John to the heavens, 'that if you have weights in your hands you can jump these little eminences much more easily. I suppose one hand alone doesn't do. What a pity he didn't tell me before—I would have lent him another bag with pleasure.'

'Nobody likes blackberries more than I do,' said John. 'But even I would hesitate to come out here on a hot afternoon and fill a great brown bag with blackberries, and then carry them eight miles home. Besides, it looks rather greedy... I beg your pardon, my lad, I didn't understand. You are taking them home to your aged mother? Of course, of course. Very commendable. If I had a penny, I would lend it to you. No, I only have a sixpence on me, and I have to give that to the little fellow who is carrying my bag over the cliffs for me... Yes, I picked him up about a couple of miles back. He has mud all up his trousers, I know.'

'Half an hour more,' I told myself, and went on doggedly, my right shoulder on fire.

'Dear, dear,' he said solicitously, 'how lopsided the youth of to-day is getting. Too much lawn-tennis, I suppose. How much better the simply healthy exercises of our forefathers; the weightlifting after lunch, the—'

He was silent for ten minutes, and then broke out rapturously once more.

'What a heavenly day! I AM glad we didn't bring a bag—it would have spoilt it altogether. We can easily borrow some slippers, and it will be jolly walking back by moonlight. Now, if you had had your way—'

'One minute more,' I said joyfully; 'and oh, my boy, how glad I am we brought a bag. What a splendid idea of yours! By the way, you haven't said much lately. A little tired by the walk?'

'I make it TWO minutes,' said John.

'Half a minute now... There! And may I never carry the confounded thing another yard.'

I threw the bag down and fell upon the grass. The bag rolled a yard or two away. Then it rolled another yard, slipped over the edge, and started bouncing down the cliff. Finally it leapt away from the earth altogether, and dropped two hundred feet into the sea.

'MY bag,' said John stupidly.

And that did for me altogether.

'I don't care a hang about your bag,' I cried. 'And I don't care a hang if I've lost my pyjamas and my best shoes and my only razor. And I've been through an hour's torture for nothing, and I don't mind that. But oh!—to think that you aren't going to have YOUR hour—'

'By Jove, neither I am,' said John, and he sat down and roared with laughter.

12

THE DOCTOR

His slippered feet stretched out luxuriously to the fire, Dr. Venables, of Mudford, lay back in his arm-chair and gave himself up to the delights of his Flor di Cabajo, No. 2, a box of which had been presented to him by an apparently grateful patient. It had been a busy day. He had prescribed more than half a dozen hot milk-puddings and a dozen changes of air; he had promised a score of times to look in again to-morrow; and the Widow Nixey had told him yet again, but at greater length than before, her private opinion of doctors.

Sometimes Gordon Venables wondered whether it was only for this that he had been the most notable student of his year at St. Bartholomew's. His brilliance, indeed, had caused something of a sensation in medical circles, and a remarkable career had been prophesied for him. It was Venables who had broken up one Suffrage meeting after another by throwing white mice at the women on the platform; who day after day had paraded London dressed in the costume of a brown dog, until arrested for biting an anti-vivisector in the leg. No wonder that all the prizes of the profession were announced to be within his grasp, and that when he buried himself in the little country town of Mudford he was thought to have thrown away recklessly opportunities such as were granted to few.

He had been in Mudford for five years now. An occasional paper in The Lancet on 'The Recurrence of Anthro-philomelitis in Earth-worms' kept him in touch with modern medical thought, but he could not help feeling that to some extent his powers were rusting in Mudford. As the years went on his chance of Harley Street dwindled.

'Come in,' he said in answer to a knock at the door.

The housekeeper's head appeared.

'There's been an accident, sir,' she gasped. 'Gentleman run over!'

He snatched up his stethoscope and, without even waiting to inquire where the accident was, hurried into the night. Something whispered to him that his chance had come.

After a quarter of an hour he stopped a small boy.

'Hallo, Johnny,' he said breathlessly, 'where's the accident?'

The boy looked at him with open mouth for some moments. Then he had an idea.

'Why, it's Doctor!' he said.

Dr. Venables pushed him over and ran on...

It was in the High Street that the accident had happened. Lord Lair, an eccentric old gentleman who sometimes walked when he might have driven, had, while dodging a motor-car, been run into by a child's hoop. He lay now on the pavement surrounded by a large and interested crowd.

'Look out,' shouted somebody from the outskirts; 'here comes Doctor.'

Dr. Venables pushed his way through to his patient. His long search for the scene of the accident had exhausted him bodily, but his mind was as clear as ever.

'Stand back there,' he said in an authoritative voice. Then, taking out his stethoscope, he made a rapid examination of his patient.

'Incised wound in the tibia,' he murmured to himself.

'Slight abrasion of the patella and contusion of the left ankle. The injuries are serious but not necessarily mortal. Who is he?'

The butcher, who had been sitting on the head of the fallen man, got up and disclosed the features of Lord Lair. Dr. Venables staggered back.

'His lordship!' he cried. 'He is a patient of Dr. Scott's! I have attended the client of another practitioner! Professionally I am ruined!'

Lord Lair, who was now breathing more easily, opened his eyes.

'Take me home,' he groaned.

Dr. Venables' situation was a terrible one. Medical etiquette demanded his immediate retirement from the case, but the promptings of humanity and the thought of his client's important position in the world were too strong for him. Throwing his scruples to the winds, he assisted the aged peer on to a hastily improvised stretcher and accompanied him to the Hall.

His lordship once in bed, the doctor examined him again. It was obvious immediately that there was only one hope of saving the patient's life. An injection of anthro-philomelitis must be given without loss of time.

Dr. Venables took off his coat and rolled up his sleeves. He never travelled without a small bottle of this serum in his waistcoat pocket—a serum which, as my readers know, is prepared from the earth-worm, in whose body (fortunately) large deposits of anthro-philomelitis are continually found. With help from a footman in holding down the patient, the injection was made. In less than a year Lord Lair was restored to health.

Dr. Gordon Venables' case came before the British Medical Council early in October. The counts in the indictment were two.

The first was that, 'on the 17th of June last, Dr. Gordon Venables did feloniously and with malice aforethought commit the disgusting and infamous crime of attending professionally the client of another practitioner.'

The second was that 'in the course of rendering professional services to the said client, Dr. Venables did knowingly and wittingly employ the assistance of one who was not a properly registered medical man, to wit, Thomas Boiling, footman, thereby showing himself to be a scurvy fellow of infamous morals.'

Dr. Venables decided to apologise. He also decided to send in an account to Lord Lair for two hundred and fifty guineas. He justified this to himself mainly on the ground that, according to a letter in that week's Lancet, the supply of anthro-philomelitis in earth-worms was suddenly giving out, and that it was necessary to recoup himself for the generous quantity he had injected into Lord Lair. Naturally, also, he felt that his lordship, as the author of the whole trouble, owed him something.

The Council, in consideration of his apology, dismissed the first count. On the second count, however, they struck him off the register.

It was a terrible position for a young doctor to be in, but Gordon Venables faced it like a man. With Lord Lair's fee in his pocket he came to town and took a house in Harley Street. When he had paid the first quarter's rent and the first instalment on the hired furniture, he had fifty pounds left.

Ten pounds he spent on embossed stationery.

Forty pounds he spent on postage-stamps.

For the next three months no journal was complete without a letter from 999 Harley Street, signed 'Gordon Venables,' in which the iniquity of his treatment by the British Medical Council was dwelt upon with the fervour of a man who knew his subject thoroughly; no such letter was complete without a side-reference to anthro-philomelitis (as found, happily, in earth-worms) and the anthro-philomelitis treatment (as recommended by peers). Six months previously the name of Venables had been utterly unknown to the man in the street. In three months' time it was better known...One-half of London said he was an infamous quack.

The other half of London said he was a martyred genius.

Both halves agreed that, after all, one might as well *try* this new what-you-may-call-it treatment, just to see if there was anything *in* it, don't you know.

It was only last week that Mr. Venables made an excellent speech against the super-tax.

13

ENTER BINGO

Before I introduce Bingo I must say a word for Humphrey, his sparring partner. Humphrey found himself on the top of my stocking last December, put there, I fancy, by Celia, though she says it was Father Christmas. He is a small yellow dog, with glass optics, and the label round his neck said, 'His eyes move.' When I had finished the oranges and sweets and nuts, when Celia and I had pulled the crackers, Humphrey remained over to sit on the music-stool, with the air of one playing the pianola. In this position he found his uses. There are times when a husband may legitimately be annoyed; at these times it was pleasant to kick Humphrey off his stool on to the divan, to stand on the divan and kick him on to the sofa, to stand on the sofa and kick him on to the bookcase; and then, feeling another man, to replace him on the music-stool and apologize to Celia. It was thus that he lost his tail.

Here we say good-bye to Humphrey for the present; Bingo claims our attention. Bingo arrived as an absurd little black tub of puppiness, warranted (by a pedigree as long as your arm) to grow into a Pekinese. It was Celia's idea to call him Bingo; because (a ridiculous reason) as a child she had had a poodle called Bingo. The less said about poodles the better; why rake up the past?

'If there is the slightest chance of Bingo—of this animal growing up into a poodle,' I said, 'he leaves my house at once.'

'*My* poodle,' said Celia, 'was a lovely dog.'

(Of course she was only a child then. She wouldn't know.)

'The point is this,' I said firmly, 'our puppy is meant for a Pekinese—the pedigree says so. From the look of him it will be touch and go whether he pulls it off. To call him by the name of a late poodle may just be the deciding factor. Now I hate poodles; I hate pet dogs. A Pekinese is not a pet dog; he is an undersized lion. Our puppy may grow into a small lion, or a mastiff, or anything like that; but I will *not* have him a poodle. If we call him Bingo, will you promise never to mention in his presence that you once had a—a—you know what I mean—called Bingo?'

She promised. I have forgiven her for having once loved a poodle. I beg you to forget about it. There is now only one Bingo, and he is a Pekinese puppy.

However, after we had decided to call him Bingo, a difficulty arose. Bingo's pedigree is full of names like Li Hung Chang and Sun Yat Sen; had we chosen a sufficiently Chinese name for him? Apart from what was due to his ancestors, were we encouraging him enough to grow into a Pekinese? What was there Oriental about 'Bingo'?

In itself, apparently, little. And Bingo himself must have felt this; for his tail continued to be nothing but a rat's tail, and his body to be nothing but a fat tub, and his head to be almost the head of any little puppy in the world. He felt it deeply. When I ragged him about it he tried to eat my ankles. I had only to go into the room in which he was, and murmur, 'Rat's tail,' to myself, or (more offensive still) 'Chewed string,' for him to rush at me. 'Where, O Bingo, is that delicate feather curling gracefully over the back, which was the pride and glory of thy great-grandfather? Is the caudal affix of the rodent thy apology for it?' And Bingo would whimper with shame.

Then we began to look him up in the map.

I found a Chinese town called 'Ning-po,' which strikes me as very much like 'Bing-go,' and Celia found another one called 'Yung-Ping,' which might just as well be 'Yung-Bing,' the obvious name of Bingo's heir when he has one. These facts being communicated to Bingo, his nose immediately began to go back a little and his tub to develop something of a waist. But what finally decided him was a discovery of mine made only yesterday. *There is a Japanese province called Bingo.* Japanese, not Chinese, it is true; but at least it is Oriental. In any case conceive one's pride in realizing suddenly that one has been called after a province and not after a poodle. It has determined Bingo unalterably to grow up in the right way.

You have Bingo now definitely a Pekinese. That being so, I may refer to his ancestors, always an object of veneration among these Easterns. I speak of (hats off, please!) Ch. Goodwood Lo.

Of course you know (I didn't myself till last week) that 'Ch.' stands for 'Champion.' On the male side Champion Goodwood Lo is Bingo's great-great-grandfather. On the female side the same animal is Bingo's great-grandfather. One couldn't be a poodle after that. A fortnight after Bingo came to us we found in a Pekinese book a photograph of Goodwood Lo. How proud we all were! Then we saw above it, 'Celebrities of the Past. The Late—'

Champion Goodwood Lo was no more! In one moment Bingo had lost both his great-grandfather and his great-great-grandfather!

We broke it to him as gently as possible, but the double shock was too much, and he passed the evening in acute depression. Annoyed with my tactlessness in letting him know anything about it, I kicked Humphrey off his stool. Humphrey, I forgot to say, has a squeak if kicked in the right place. He squeaked.

Bingo, at that time still uncertain of his destiny, had at least the courage of the lion. Just for a moment he hesitated. Then with a pounce he was upon Humphrey.

Till then I had regarded Humphrey—save for his power of rolling the eyes and his habit of taking long jumps from the music-stool to the book-case—as rather a sedentary character. But in the fight which followed he put up an amazingly good resistance. At one time he was underneath Bingo; the next moment he had Bingo down; first one, then the other, seemed to gain the advantage. But blood will tell. Humphrey's ancestry is unknown; I blush to say that it may possibly be German. Bingo had Goodwood Lo to support him—in two places. Gradually he got the upper hand; and at last, taking the reluctant Humphrey by the ear, he dragged him laboriously beneath the sofa. He emerged alone, with tail wagging, and was taken on to his mistress' lap. There he slept, his grief forgotten.

So Humphrey was found a job. Whenever Bingo wants exercise, Humphrey plants himself in the middle of the room, his eyes cast upwards in an affectation of innocence. 'I'm just sitting here,' says Humphrey; 'I believe there's a fly on the ceiling.' It is a challenge which no great-grandson of Goodwood Lo could resist. With a rush Bingo is at him. 'I'll learn you to stand in my way,' he splutters. And the great dust-up begins...

Brave little Bingo! I don't wonder that so warlike a race as the Japanese has called a province after him.

14

THE FATAL GIFT

People say to me sometimes, 'Oh, you know Woolman, don't you?' I acknowledge that I do, and, after the silence that always ensues, I add, 'If you want to say anything against him, please go on.' You can almost hear the sigh of relief that goes up. 'I thought he was a friend of yours,' they say cheerfully. 'But, of course, if—' and then they begin.

I think it is time I explained my supposed friendship for Ernest Merrowby Woolman—confound him.

The affair began in a taxicab two years ago. Andrew had been dining with me that night; we walked out to the cab-rank together; I told the driver where to go, and Andrew stepped in, waved good-bye to me from the window, and sat down suddenly upon something hard. He drew it from beneath him, and found it was an extremely massive (and quite new) silver cigar-case. He put it in his pocket with the intention of giving it to the driver when he got out, but quite naturally forgot. Next morning he found it on his dressing-table. So he put it in his pocket again, meaning to leave it at Scotland Yard on his way to the City.

Next morning it was on his dressing-table again.

This went on for some days. After a week or so Andrew saw that it was hopeless to try to get a cigar-case back to

Scotland Yard in this casual sort of way; it must be taken there deliberately by somebody who had a morning to spare and was willing to devote it to this special purpose. He placed the case, therefore, prominently on a small table in the dining-room to await the occasion; calling also the attention of his family to it, as an excuse for an outing when they were not otherwise engaged.

At times he used to say, 'I must really take that cigar-case to Scotland Yard to-morrow.'

At other times he would say, 'Somebody must really take that cigar-case to Scotland Yard to-day.'

And so the weeks rolled on...

It was about a year later that I first got mixed up with the thing. I must have dined with the Andrews several times without noticing the cigar-case, but on this occasion it caught my eye as we wandered out to join the ladies, and I picked it up carelessly. Well, not exactly carelessly; it was too heavy for that.

'Why didn't you tell me,' I said, 'that you had stood for Parliament and that your supporters had consoled you with a large piece of plate? Hallo, they've put the wrong initials on it. How unbusiness-like.'

'Oh, that?' said Andrew. 'Is it still there?'

'Why not? It's quite a solid little table. But you haven't explained why your constituents, who must have seen your name on hundreds of posters, thought your initials were E.M.W.'

Andrew explained.

'Then it isn't yours at all?' I said in amazement.

'Of course, not.'

'But, my dear man, this is theft. Stealing by finding, they call it. You could get.' I looked at him almost with admiration, 'you could get two years for this'; and I weighed the cigar-case in my hand. 'I believe you're the only one of my friends who could be certain of two years,' I went on musingly. 'Let's see, there's—'

'Nonsense,' said Andrew uneasily. 'But still, perhaps I'd better take it back to Scotland Yard to-morrow.'

'And tell them you've kept it for a year? They'd run you in at once. No, what you want to do is to get rid of it without their knowledge. But how—that's the question. You can't give it away because of the initials.'

'It's easy enough. I can leave it in another cab, or drop it in the river.'

'Andrew, Andrew,' I cried, 'you're determined to go to prison! Don't you know from all the humorous articles you've ever read that, if you try to lose anything, then you never can? It's one of the stock remarks one makes to women in the endeavour to keep them amused. No, you must think of some more subtle way of disposing of it.'

'I'll pretend it's yours,' said Andrew more subtly, and he placed it in my pocket.

'No, you don't,' I said. 'But I tell you what I will do. I'll take it for a week and see if I can get rid of it. If I can't, I shall give it you back and wash my hands of the whole business—except, of course, for the monthly letter or whatever it is they allow you at the Scrubbs. You may still count on me for that.'

And then the extraordinary thing happened. The next morning I received a letter from a stranger, asking for some simple information which I could have given him on a post-card. And so I should have done—or possibly, I am afraid, have forgotten to answer at all—but for the way that the letter ended up.

'Yours very truly,
ERNEST M. WOOLMAN.'

The magic initials! It was a chance not to be missed. I wrote enthusiastically back and asked him to lunch.

He came. I gave him all the information he wanted, and more. Whether he was a pleasant sort of person or not I hardly noticed; I was so very pleasant myself.

He returned my enthusiasm. He asked me to dine with him the following week. A little party at the Savoy—his birthday, you know.

I accepted gladly. I rolled up at the party with my little present...a massive silver cigar-case...suitably engraved.

So there you are. He clings to me. He seems to have formed the absurd idea that I am fond of him. A few months after that evening at the Savoy he was married. I was invited to the wedding—confound him. Of course I had to live up to my birthday present; the least I could do was an enormous silver cigar-box (not engraved), which bound me to him still more strongly.

By that time I realized that I hated him. He was pushing, familiar, everything that I disliked. All my friends wondered how I had become so intimate with him...

Well, now they know. And the original E.M.W., if he has the sense to read this, also knows. If he cares to prosecute Ernest Merrowby Woolman for being in possession of stolen goods, I shall be glad to give him any information. Woolman is generally to be found leaving my rooms at about 6.30 in the evening, and a smart detective could easily nab him as he steps out.

15

THE COMPLETE KITCHEN

I sat in the drawing-room after dinner with my knees together and my hands in my lap, and waited for the game to be explained to me.

'There's a pencil for you,' said somebody.

'Thank you very much,' I said and put it carefully away. Evidently I had won a forfeit already. It wasn't a very good pencil, though.

'Now, has everybody got pencils?' asked somebody else. 'The game is called "Furnishing a Kitchen." It's quite easy. Will somebody think of a letter?' She turned to me. 'Perhaps you'd better.'

'Certainly,' I said, and I immediately thought very hard of N. These thought-reading games are called different things, but they are all the same, really, and I don't believe in any of them.

'Well?' said everybody.

'What?... Yes, I have. Go on... Oh, I beg your pardon,' I said in confusion. 'I thought you—N is the letter.'

'N or M?'

I smiled knowingly to myself.

'My godfather and my godmother,' I went on cautiously—

'It was N,' interrupted somebody. 'Now then, you've got five minutes in which to write down everything you can beginning with N. Go.' And they all started to write like anything.

I took my pencil out and began to think. I know it sounds an easy game to you now, as you sit at your desk surrounded by dictionaries; but when you are squeezed on to the edge of a sofa, given a very blunt pencil and a thin piece of paper, and challenged to write in five minutes (on your knees) all the words you can think of beginning with a certain letter—well, it is another matter altogether. I thought of no end of things which started with K, or even L; I thought of 'rhinoceros' which is a very long word and starts with R; but as for—

I looked at my watch and groaned. One minute gone.

'I must keep calm,' I said and in a bold hand I wrote *Napoleon*. Then after a moment's thought, I added *Nitroglycerine*, and *Nats*.

'This is splendid,' I told myself. '*Nottingham, Nobody* and *Noon*. That makes six.'

At six I stuck for two minutes. I did worse than that in fact; for I suddenly remembered that gnats were spelt with a G. However, I decided to leave them, in case nobody else remembered. And on the fourth minute I added *Non-sequitur*.

'Time!' said somebody.

'Just a moment,' said everybody. They wrote down another word or two (which isn't fair), and then began to add up. 'I've got thirty,' said one.

'Thirty-two.'

'Twenty-five.'

'Good Heavens,' I said, 'I've only got seven.'

There was a shout of laughter.

'Then you'd better begin,' said somebody. 'Read them out.'

I coughed nervously, and began.

'Napoleon.'

There was another shout of laughter.

'I am afraid we can't allow that.'

'Why ever not?' I asked in amazement.

'Well, you'd hardly find him in a kitchen, would you?'

I took out a handkerchief and wiped my brow. 'I don't want to find him in a kitchen,' I said nervously. 'Why should I? As a matter of fact he's dead. I don't see what the kitchen's got to do with it. Kitchens begin with a K.'

'But the game is called "Furnishing a Kitchen." You have to make a list of things beginning with N which you would find in a kitchen. You understood that, didn't you?'

'Y-y-yes,' I said. 'Oh, y-y-y-yes. Of course.'

'So Napoleon—'

I pulled myself together with a great effort.

'You don't understand,' I said with dignity. 'The cook's name was Napoleon.'

'Cooks aren't called Napoleon,' said everybody.

'This one was. Carrie Napoleon. Her mistress was just as surprised at first as you were, but Carrie assured her that—'

'No, I'm afraid we can't allow it.'

'I'm sorry,' I said; 'I'm wrong about that. Her name was Carrie Smith. But her young man was a soldier, and she had bought a Life of Napoleon for a birthday present for him. It stood on the dresser waiting for her next Sunday out.'

'Oh! Oh, well, I suppose that is possible. Go on.'

'Gnats,' I went on nervously and hastily. 'Of course I know that—'

'Gnats are spelt with a G,' they shrieked.

'These weren't. They had lost the G when they were quite young, and consequently couldn't bite at all, and Cook said that—'

'No; I'm afraid not.'

'I'm sorry,' I said resignedly. 'I had about forty of them—on the dresser. If you won't allow any of them, it pulls me down a lot. Er—then we have Nitro-glycerine.'

There was another howl of derision.

'Not at all,' I said haughtily. 'Cook had chapped hands very badly, and she went to the chemist's one evening for a little glycerine. The chemist was out, and his assistant—a very nervous young fellow—gave her nitro-glycerine by mistake. It stood on the dresser, it did, really.'

'Well,' said everybody very reluctantly, 'I suppose—'

I went on hastily.

'That's two. Then Nobody. Of course, you might easily find nobody in the kitchen. In fact you would pretty often, I should say. Three. The next is Noon. It could be noon in the kitchen as well as anywhere else. Don't be narrow-minded about that.'

'All right. Go on.'

'Non-sequitur,' I said doubtfully.

'What on earth—'

'It's a little difficult to explain, but the idea is this. At most restaurants you can get a second help of anything for half-price, and that is technically called a "follow." Now, if they didn't give you a follow, that would be a Non-sequitur... You do see that, don't you?'

There was a deadly silence.

'Five,' I said cheerfully. 'The last is Nottingham. I must confess,' I added magnanimously, 'that I am a bit doubtful whether you would actually find Nottingham in a kitchen.'

'You don't say so!'

'Yes. My feeling is that you would be more likely to find the kitchen in Nottingham. On the other hand, it is just possible that as Calais was found engraven on Mary's heart, so—Oh, very well. Then it remains at five.'

◆

Of course you think that as I only had five, I came out last. But you are wrong. There is a pleasing rule in this game that, if you have any word in your list which somebody else has, you cannot count it. And as all the others had the obvious things—such as a nutmeg-grater or a neck of mutton, or a nomlette—my five won easily. And you will note that if only I had been allowed to count my gnats, it would have been forty-five.

16

GETTING MARRIED

I—The day

Probably you thought that getting married was quite a simple business. So did I. We were both wrong; it is the very dickens. Of course, I am not going to draw back now. As I keep telling Celia, her Ronald is a man of powerful fibre, and when he says he will do a thing he does it—eventually. She shall have her wedding all right; I have sworn it. But I do wish that there weren't so many things to be arranged first.

The fact that we had to fix a day was broken to me one afternoon when Celia was showing me to some relatives of hers in the Addison Road. I got entangled with an elderly cousin on the hearth-rug; and though I know nothing about motor-bicycles I talked about them for several hours under the impression that they were his subject. It turned out afterwards that he was equally ignorant of them, but thought they were mine. Perhaps we shall get on better at a second meeting. However, just when we were both thoroughly sick of each other, Celia broke off her gay chat with an aunt to say to me:

'By the way, Ronald, we did settle on the eleventh, didn't we?'

I looked at her blankly, my mind naturally full of motor-bicycles.

'The wedding,' smiled Celia.

'Right-o,' I said with enthusiasm. I was glad to be assured that I should not go on talking about motor-bicycles for ever, and that on the eleventh, anyhow, there would be a short interruption for the ceremony. Feeling almost friendly to the cousin, I plunged into his favourite subject again.

On the way home Celia returned to the matter.

'Or you would rather it was the twelfth?' she asked.

'I've never heard a word about this before,' I said. 'It all comes as a surprise to me.'

'Why, I'm always asking you.'

'Well, it's very forward of you, and I don't know what young people are coming to nowadays. Celia, what's the good of my talking to your cousin for three hours about motor-bicycling? Surely one can get married just as well without that?'

'One can't get married without settling the day,' said Celia, coming cleverly back to the point.

Well, I suppose one can't. But somehow I had expected to be spared all this bother. I think my idea was that Celia would say to me suddenly one evening, 'By the way, Ronald, don't forget we're being married to-morrow,' and I should have said 'Where?' And on being told the time and place, I should have turned up pretty punctually; and after my best man had told me where to stand, and the clergyman had told me what to say, and my solicitor had told me where to sign my name, we should have driven from the church a happy married couple... and in the carriage Celia would have told me where we were spending the honeymoon.

However, it was not to be so.

'All right, the eleventh,' I said. 'Any particular month?'

'No,' smiled Celia, 'just any month. Or, if you like, every month.'

'The eleventh of June,' I surmised. 'It is probably the one

day in the year on which my Uncle Thomas cannot come. But no matter. The eleventh let it be.'

'Then that's settled. And at St. Miriam's?'

For some reason Celia has set her heart on St. Miriam's. Personally I have no feeling about it. St. Andrew's-by-the-Wardrobe or St. Bartholomew's-Without would suit me equally well.

'All right,' I said, 'St. Miriam's.'

There, you might suppose, the matter would have ended; but no.

'Then you will see about it to-morrow?' said Celia persuasively.

I was appalled at the idea.

'Surely,' I said, 'this is for you, or your father, or...or somebody to arrange.'

'Of course it's for the bridegroom,' protested Celia.

'In theory, perhaps. But anyhow not the bridegroom personally. His best man...or his solicitor...or...I mean, you're not suggesting that I myself—Oh, well, if you insist. Still, I must say I don't see what's the good of having a best man *and* a solicitor if—Oh, all right, Celia, I'll go to-morrow.'

So I went. For half an hour I padded round St. Miriam's nervously, and then summoning up all my courage, I knocked my pipe out and entered.

'I want,' I said jauntily to a sexton or a sacristan or something—'I want—er—a wedding.' And I added, 'For two.'

He didn't seem as nervous as I was. He enquired quite calmly when I wanted it.

'The eleventh of June,' I said. 'It's probably the one day in the year on which my Uncle Thomas—However, that wouldn't interest you. The point is that it's the eleventh.'

The clerk consulted his wedding-book. Then he made the surprising announcement that the only day he could offer me in June was the seventeenth. I was amazed.

'I am a very old customer,' I said reproachfully. 'I mean, I have often been to your church in my time. Surely—'

'We've weddings fixed on all the other days.'

'Yes, yes, but you could persuade somebody to change his day, couldn't you? Or if he is very much set on being married on the eleventh you might recommend some other church to him. I daresay you know of some good ones. You see, Celia—my—that is, we're particularly keen, for some reason, on St. Miriam's.'

The clerk didn't appreciate my suggestion. He insisted that the seventeenth was the only day.

'Then will you have the seventeenth?' he asked.

'My dear fellow, I can't possibly say off-hand,' I protested. 'I am not alone in this. I have a friend with me. I will go back and tell her what you say. She may decide to withdraw her offer altogether.'

I went back and told Celia.

'Bother,' she said. 'What shall we do?'

'There are other churches. There's your own, for example.'

'Yes, but you know I don't like that. Why shouldn't we be married on the seventeenth?'

'I don't know at all. It seems an excellent day; it lets in my Uncle Thomas. Of course, it may exclude my Uncle William, but one can't have everything.'

'Then will you go and fix it for the seventeenth to-morrow?'

'Can't I send my solicitor this time?' I asked. 'Of course, if you particularly want me to go myself, I will. But really, dear, I seem to be living at St. Miriam's nowadays.'

And even that wasn't the end of the business. For, just as I was leaving her, Celia broke it to me that St. Miriam's was neither in her parish nor in mine, and that, in order to qualify as a bridegroom, I should have to hire a room somewhere near.

'But I am very comfortable where I am,' I assured her.

'You needn't live there, Ronald. You only want to leave a hat there, you know.'

'Oh, very well,' I sighed.

She came to the hall with me; and, having said good-bye to her, I repeated my lesson.

'The seventeenth, fix it up to-morrow, take a room near St. Miriam's, and leave a hat there. Good-bye.'

'Good-bye... And oh, Ronald!' She looked at me critically as I stood in the doorway. 'You might leave that one,' she said.

'By the way,' said Celia suddenly, 'what have you done about the fixtures?'

'Nothing,' I replied truthfully.

'Well, we must do something about them.'

'Yes. My solicitor—he shall do something about them. Don't let's talk about them now. I've only got three hours more with you, and then I must dash back to my work.'

I must say that any mention of fixtures has always bored me intensely. When it was a matter of getting a house to live in I was all energy. As soon as Celia had found it, I put my solicitor on to it; and within a month I had signed my name in two places, and was the owner of a highly residential flat in the best part of the neighbourhood. But my effort so exhausted me that I have felt utterly unable since to cope with the question of the curtain-rod in the bathroom or whatever it is that Celia means by fixtures. These things will arrange themselves somehow, I feel confident.

Meanwhile the decorators are hard at work. A thrill of pride inflates me when I think of the decorators at work. I don't know how they got there; I suppose I must have ordered them. Celia says that *she* ordered them and chose all the papers herself, and that all I did was to say that the papers she had chosen were very pretty; but this doesn't sound like me in the least. I am convinced that I was the man of action when it came to ordering decorators.

'And now,' said Celia one day, 'we can go and choose the electric-light fittings.'

'Celia,' I said in admiration, 'you're a wonderful person. I should have forgotten all about them.'

'Why, they're about the most important thing in the flat.'

'Somehow I never regarded anybody as choosing them. I thought they just grew in the wall. From bulbs.'

When we got into the shop Celia became businesslike at once.

'We'd better start with the hall,' she told the man.

'Everybody else will have to,' I said, 'so we may as well.'

'What sort of a light did you want there?' he asked.

'A strong one,' I said; 'so as to be able to watch our guests carefully when they pass the umbrella-stand.'

Celia waved me away and explained that we wanted a hanging lantern. It appeared that this shop made a speciality not so much of the voltage as of the lamps enclosing it.

'How do you like that?' asked the man, pointing to a magnificent affair in brass. He wandered off to a switch, and turned it on.

'Dare you ask him the price?' I asked Celia. 'It looks to me about a thousand pounds. If it is, say that you don't like the style. Don't let him think we can't afford it.'

'Yes,' said Celia, in a careless sort of way. 'I'm not sure that I care about that. How much is it?'

'Two pounds.'

I was not going to show my relief. 'Without the light, of course?' I said disparagingly.

'How do you think it would look in the hall?' said Celia to me.

'I think our guests would be encouraged to proceed. They'd

see that we were pretty good people.'

'I don't like it. It's too ornate.'

'Then show us something less ornate,' I told the man sternly.

He showed us things less ornate. At the end of an hour Celia said she thought we'd better get on to another room, and come back to the hall afterwards. We decided to proceed to the drawing-room.

'We must go all out over these,' said Celia; 'I want these to be really beautiful.'

At the end of another hour Celia said she thought we'd better get on to my workroom. My workroom, as the name implies, is the room to which I am to retire when I want complete quiet. Sometimes I shall go there after lunch...and have it.

'We can come back to the drawing-room afterwards,' she said. 'It's really very important that we should get the right ones for that. Your room won't be so difficult, but, of course, you must have awfully nice ones.'

I looked at my watch.

'It's a quarter to one,' I said. 'At 2.15 on the seventeenth of June we are due at St. Miriam's. If you think we shall have bought anything by then, let's go on. If, as seems to me, there is no hope at all, then let's have lunch to-day anyhow. After lunch we may be able to find some way out of the *impasse*.'

After lunch I had an idea.

'This afternoon,' I said, 'we will begin to get some furniture together.'

'But what about the electric fittings? We must finish off those.'

'This is an experiment. I want to see if we can buy a chest of drawers. It may just be our day for it.'

'And we settle the fittings to-morrow. Yes?'

'I don't know. We may not want them. It all depends on whether we can buy a chest of drawers this afternoon. If we can't, then I don't see how we can ever be married on the seventeenth of June. Somebody's got to be, because I've engaged the church. The question is whether it's going to be us. Let's go and buy a chest of drawers this afternoon, and see.'

The old gentleman in the little shop Celia knew of was delighted to see us.

'Chestesses? Ah, you 'ave come to the right place.' He led the way into the depths. 'There now. There's a chest—real old, that is.' He gave it a hearty smack. 'You don't see a chest like that nowadays. They can't *make* 'em. Three pound ten. You couldn't have got that to-morrer. I'd have sold it for four pound to-morrer.'

'I knew it was our day,' I said.

'Real old, that is. Spanish me'ogany, all oak lined. That's right, sir, pull the drawers out and see for yourself. Let the lady see. There's no imitation there, lady. A real old chest, that is. Come in 'ere in a week and you'd have to pay five pounds for it. Me'ogany's going up, you see, that's how.'

'Well?' I said to Celia.

'It's perfectly sweet. Hadn't we better see some more?'

We saw two more. Both of them Spanish me'ogany, oak lined, pull-the-drawers-out-and-see-for-yourself-lady. Half an hour passed rapidly.

'Well?' I said.

'I really don't know which I like best. Which do you?'

'The first; it's nearer the door.'

'There's another shop just over the way. We'd better just look there too, and then we can come back to decide to-morrow.'

We went out. I glanced at my watch. It was 3.30, and we were being married at 2.15 on the seventeenth of June.

'Wait a moment,' I said, 'I've forgotten my gloves.'

I may be a slow starter, but I am very firm when roused. I went into the shop, wrote a cheque for the three chests of drawers, and told the man where to send them. When I returned, Celia was at the shop opposite, pulling the drawers out of a real old mahogany chest which was standing on the pavement outside.

'This is even better,' she said. 'It's perfectly adorable. I wonder if it's more expensive.'

'I'll just ask,' I said.

I went in and, without an unnecessary word, bought that chest too. Then I came back to Celia. It was 3.45, and on the seventeenth of June at 2.15—Well, we had four chests of drawers towards it.

'Celia,' I said, 'we may just do it yet.'

'I know I oughtn't to be dallying here,' I said; 'I ought to be doing something strenuous in preparation for the wedding. Counting the bells at St. Miriam's, or varnishing the floors in the flat, or—Tell me what I ought to be doing, Celia, and I'll go on not doing it for a bit.'

'There's the honeymoon,' said Celia.

'I knew there was something.'

'Do tell me what you're doing about it?'

'Thinking about it.'

'You haven't written to any one about rooms yet?'

'Celia,' I said reproachfully, 'you seem to have forgotten why I am marrying you.'

When Celia was browbeaten into her present engagement, she said frankly that she was only consenting to marry me because of my pianola, which she had always coveted. In return I pointed out that I was only asking her to marry me because I wanted somebody to write my letters. There opened before me, in that glad moment, a vista of invitations and accounts-rendered all answered promptly by Celia, instead of put off till next month by me. It was a wonderful vision to one who (very properly) detests letter-writing. And yet, here she was, even before the ceremony, expecting me to enter into a deliberate correspondence with all sorts of strange people who as yet had not come into my life at all. It was too much.

'We will get,' I said, 'your father to write some letters for us.'

'But what's he got to do with it?'

'I don't want to complain of your father, Celia, but it seems to me that he is not doing his fair share. There ought to be a certain give-and-take in the matter. *I* find you a nice church to be married in—good. *He* finds you a nice place to honeymoon in—excellent. After all, you are still his daughter.'

'All right,' said Celia, 'I'll ask father to do it. "Dear Mrs. Bunn, my little boy wants to spend his holidays with you in June. I am writing to ask you if you will take care of him and see that he doesn't do anything dangerous. He has a nice disposition, but wants watching."' She patted my head gently. 'Something like that.'

I got up and went to the writing-desk.

'I can see I shall have to do it myself,' I sighed. 'Give me the address and I'll begin.'

'But we haven't quite settled where we're going yet, have we?'

I put the pen down thankfully and went back to the sofa.

'Good! Then I needn't write to-day, anyhow. It is wonderful, dear, how difficulties roll away when you face them. Almost at once we arrive at the conclusion that I needn't write to-day. Splendid! Well, where shall we go? This will want a lot of thought. Perhaps,' I added, 'I needn't write to-morrow.'

'We had almost fixed on England, hadn't we?'

'Somebody was telling me that Lynton was very beautiful.

I should like to go to Lynton.'

'But *every one* goes to Lynton for their honeymoon.'

'Then let's be original and go to Birmingham. "The happy couple left for Birmingham, where the honeymoon will be spent." Sensation.'

'"The bride left the train at Ealing." More sensation.'

'I think the great thing,' I said, trying to be businesslike, 'is to fix the county first. If we fixed on Rutland, then the rest would probably be easy.'

'The great thing,' said Celia, 'is to decide what we want. Sea, or river, or mountains, or—or golf.'

At the word golf I coughed and looked out of the window.

Now I am very fond of Celia—I mean of golf, and—what I really mean, of course, is that I am very fond of both of them. But I do think that on a honeymoon Celia should come first. After all, I shall have plenty of other holidays for golf... although, of course, three weeks in the summer without any golf at all—Still, I think Celia should come first.

'Our trouble,' I said to her, 'is that neither of us has ever been on a honeymoon before, and so we've no idea what it will be like. After all, why should we get bored with each other? Surely we don't depend on golf to amuse us?'

'All the same, I think your golf *would* amuse me,' said Celia. 'Besides, I want you to be as happy as you possibly can be.'

'Yes, but supposing I was slicing my drives all the time, I should be miserable. I should be torn between the desire to go back to London and have a lesson with the professional and the desire to stay on honeymooning with you. One can't be happy in a quandary like that.'

'Very well then, no golf. Settled?'

'Quite. Now then, let's decide about the scenery. What sort of soil do you prefer?'

When I left Celia that day we had agreed on this much:

that we wouldn't bother about golf, and that the mountains, rivers, valleys, and so on should be left entirely to nature. All we were to enquire for was (in the words of an advertisement Celia had seen) 'a perfect spot for a honeymoon.'

In the course of the next day I heard of seven spots; varying from a spot in Surrey 'dotted with firs,' to a dot in the Pacific spotted with—I forget what, natives probably. Taken together they were the seven only possible spots for a honeymoon.

'We shall have to have seven honeymoons,' I said to Celia when I had told her my news. 'One honeymoon, one spot.'

'Wait,' she said. 'I have heard of an ideal spot.'

'Speaking as a spot expert, I don't think that's necessarily better than an only possible spot,' I objected. 'Still, tell me about it.'

'Well, to begin with, it's close to the sea.'

'So we can bathe when we're bored. Good.'

'And it's got a river, if you want to fish—'

'I don't. I should hate to catch a fish who was perhaps on his honeymoon too. Still, I like the idea of a river.'

'And quite a good mountain, and lovely walks, and, in fact, everything. Except a picture-palace, luckily.'

'It sounds all right,' I said doubtfully. 'We might just spend the next day or two thinking about my seven spots, and then I might...possibly...feel strong enough to write.'

'Oh, I nearly forgot. I *have* written, Ronald.'

'You have?' I cried. 'Then, my dear, what else matters? It's a perfect spot.' I lay back in relief. 'And there, thank 'evings, is another thing settled. Bless you.'

'Yes. And, by the way, there *is* golf quite close too. But that,' she smiled, 'needn't prevent us going there.'

'Of course not. We shall just ignore the course.'

'Perhaps, so as to be on the safe side, you'd better leave your clubs behind.'

'Perhaps I'd better,' I said carelessly.

All the same I don't think I will. One never knows what may happen...and at the outset of one's matrimonial career to have to go to the expense of an entirely new set of clubs would be a most regrettable business.

'I suppose,' I said, 'it's too late to cancel this wedding now?'

'Well,' said Celia, 'the invitations are out, and the presents are pouring in, and mother's just ordered the most melting dress for herself that you ever saw. Besides, who's to live in the flat if we don't?'

'There's a good deal in what you say. Still, I am alarmed, seriously alarmed. Look here.' I drew out a printed slip and flourished it before her.

'Not a writ? My poor Ronald!'

'Worse than that. This is the St. Miriam's bill of fare for weddings. Celia, I had no idea marriage was so expensive. I thought one rolled-gold ring would practically see it.'

It was a formidable document. Starting with 'full choir and organ' which came to a million pounds, and working down through 'boys' voices only,' and 'red carpet' to 'policemen for controlling traffic—per policeman, 5s.,' it included altogether some two dozen ways of disposing of my savings.

'If we have the whole *menu*,' I said, 'I shall be ruined. You wouldn't like to have a ruined husband.'

Celia took the list and went through it carefully.

'I might say "Season,"' I suggested, 'or "Press."'

'Well, to begin with,' said Celia, 'we needn't have a full choir.'

'Need we have an organ or a choir at all? In thanking people for their kind presents you might add, "By the way, do you sing?" Then we could arrange to have all the warblers in the front. My best man or my solicitor could give the note.'

'Boys' voices only,' decided Celia. 'Then what about bells?'

'I should like some nice bells. If the price is "per bell" we might give an order for five good ones.'

'Let's do without bells. You see, they don't begin to ring till we've left the church, so they won't be any good to *us*.'

This seemed to me an extraordinary line to take.

'My dear child,' I remonstrated, 'the whole thing is being got up not for ourselves, but for our guests. We shall be much too preoccupied to appreciate any of the good things we provide— the texture of the red carpet or the quality of the singing. I dreamt last night that I quite forgot about the wedding-ring till 1.30 on the actual day, and the only cab I could find to take me to a jeweller's was drawn by a camel. Of course, it may not turn out to be as bad as that, but it will certainly be an anxious afternoon for both of us. And so we must consider the entertainment entirely from the point of view of our guests. Whether their craving is for champagne or bells, it must be satisfied.'

'I'm sure they'll be better without bells. Because when the policemen call out "Mr. Spifkins" carriage,' Mr. Spifkins mightn't hear if there were a lot of bells clashing about.'

'Very well, no bells. But, mind you,' I said sternly, 'I shall insist on a clergyman.'

We went through the rest of the *menu*, course by course.

'I know what I shall do,' I said at last. 'I shall call on my friend the Clerk again, and I shall speak to him quite frankly. I shall say, "Here is a cheque for a thousand pounds. It is all I can afford—and, by the way, you'd better pay it in quickly or it will be dishonoured. Can you do us up a nice wedding for a thousand inclusive?"'

'Like the Christmas hampers at the stores.'

'Exactly. A dozen boys' voices, a half-dozen of bells, ten yards of awning, and twenty-four oranges, or vergers, or whatever it is. We ought to get a nice parcel for a thousand pounds.'

'Or,' said Celia, 'we might send the list round to our friends as suggestions for wedding presents. I'm sure Jane would love to give us a couple of policemen.'

'We'd much better leave the whole thing to your father. I incline more and more to the opinion that it is *his* business to provide the wedding. I must ask my solicitor about it.'

'He's providing the bride.'

'Yes, but I think he might go further. I can't help feeling that the bells would come very well from him. "Bride's father to bridegroom—A peal of bells." People would think it was something in silver for the hall. It would do him a lot of good in business circles.'

'And that reminds me,' smiled Celia, 'there's been some talk about a present from Miss Popley.'

I have come to the conclusion that it is impossible to get married decently unless one's life is ordered on some sort of system. Mine never has been; and the result is that I make terrible mistakes—particularly in the case of Miss Popley. At the beginning of the business, when the news got round to Miss Popley, I received from her a sweet letter of congratulation. Knowing that she was rather particular in these matters I braced myself up and thanked her heartily by return of post. Three days later, when looking for a cheque I had lost, I accidentally came across her letter. 'Help, help!' I cried. 'This came days ago, and I haven't answered yet.' I sat down at once and thanked her enthusiastically. Another week passed and I began to feel that I must really make an effort to catch my correspondence up; so I got out all my letters of congratulation of the last ten days and devoted an afternoon to answering them. I used much the same form of thanks in all of them…with the exception of Miss Popley's, which was phrased particularly warmly.

So much for that. But Miss Popley is Celia's dear friend also. When I made out my list of guests I included Miss Popley; so, in her list, did Celia. The result was that Miss Popley received two invitations to the wedding... Sometimes I fear she must think we are pursuing her.

'What does she say about a present?' I asked.

'She wants us to tell her what we want.'

'What are we to say? If we said an elephant—'

'With a small card tied on to his ear, and "Best wishes from Miss Popley" on it. It would look heavenly among the other presents.'

'You see what I mean, Celia. Are we to suggest something worth a thousand pounds, or something worth ninepence? It's awfully kind of her, but it makes it jolly difficult for us.'

'Something that might cost anything from ninepence to a thousand pounds,' suggested Celia.

'Then that washes out the elephant.'

'Can't you get the ninepenny ones now?'

'I suppose,' I said, reverting to the subject which most weighed on me, 'she wouldn't like to give the men's voices for the choir?'

'No, I think a clock,' said Celia. 'A clock can cost anything you like—or don't like.'

'Right-o. And perhaps we'd better settle now. When it comes, how many times shall we write and thank her for it?'

Celia considered. 'Four times, I think,' she said.

Well, as Celia says, it's too late to draw back now. But I shall be glad when it's all over. As I began by saying, there's too much 'arranging' and 'settling' and 'fixing' about the thing for me. In the necessary negotiations and preparations I fear I have not shone. And so I shall be truly glad when we have settled down in our flat...and Celia can restore my confidence in myself once more by talking loudly to her domestic staff about 'The Master.'

17

POOH GETS STUCK IN RABBIT'S HOLE

Christopher Robin nodded. 'Then there's only one thing to be done,' he said. 'We shall have to wait for you to get thin again.' 'How long does getting thin take?' asked Pooh anxiously. 'About a week I should think.' 'But I can't stay here for a week!' 'You can stay here all right, silly old Bear. It's getting you out which is so difficult.' 'We'll read to you,' said Rabbit cheerfully. 'And I hope it won't snow,' he added. 'And I say, old fellow, you're taking up a good deal of room in my house—do you mind if I use your back legs as a towel-horse? Because, I mean, there they are—doing nothing—and it would be very convenient just to hang the towels on them.' 'A week!' said Pooh gloomily. 'What about meals?' 'I'm afraid no meals,' said Christopher Robin, 'because of getting thin quicker. But we will read to you.' Bear began to sigh, and then found he couldn't because he was so tightly stuck; and a tear rolled down his eye, as he said: 'Then would you read a Sustaining Book, such as would help and comfort a Wedged Bear in Great Tightness?' So for a week Christopher Robin read that sort of book at the North end of Pooh, and Rabbit hung his washing on the South end... and in between Bear felt himself getting slenderer and slenderer. And at the end of the week Christopher Robin said, 'Now!'

So he took hold of Pooh's front paws and Rabbit took hold of Christopher Robin, and all Rabbit's friends and relations took hold of Rabbit, and they all pulled together. And for a long time Pooh only said, 'Ow!' And, 'Oh!' And then, all of a sudden he said, 'Pop!' just if a cork were coming out of a bottle. And Christopher Robin and Rabbit and all relations went head-over-heels backwards...and on top of them came Winnie-the-Pooh free! So with a nod of thanks to his friends, he went on with his walk through the forest, humming proudly to himself. But Christopher Robin looked after him lovingly, and said to himself, 'Silly Old Bear!'

18

TIGGERS DON'T CLIMB TREES

O f course they can. Tiggers can do everything.' 'Can they climb trees better then Pooh?' asked Roo, stopping under the tallest Pine Tree, and looking up at it. 'Climbing trees is what they do the best,' said Tigger. 'Much better then Poohs.' 'Could they climb this one?' 'They're always climb trees like that,' said Tigger. 'Up and down all day.' 'Oo Tigger, are they really?' 'I'll show you,' said Tigger bravely, 'and you can sit on my back and watch me.' For all the things which he had said Tiggers could do, the only one he felt really certain about suddenly was climbing trees.

'Oo, Tigger-oo, Tigger-oo. Tigger!' squeaked Roo excitedly. So he sat on Tigger's back and up they went. And for the first ten feet Tigger said happily to himself, 'Up we go!' And for the next ten feet he said: 'I always said Tiggers could climb trees.' And for the next ten feet he said, 'Not that it's easy, mind you.' And for the next ten feet he said: 'Of course, there's the coming down too. Backwards.' And then he said: 'Which will be difficult...' 'Unless one fell...' 'When it would be...' 'EASY.'

And at the word 'easy', the branch he was standing on broke suddenly and he just managed to clutch at the one above him as he felt himself going...and then slowly he got his chin over it...and then one back paw...and then the other...until at last he was sitting on it, breathing very quickly, and wishing that he gone for swimming instead. Roo climbed off, and sat down next to him. 'Oo, Tigger,' he said excitedly, 'are we at the top?' 'No,' said tigger. 'Are we going to the top?' 'NO,' said Tigger...

'There's something in one of the Pine Trees.' 'So there is!' said Pooh, looking up wonderingly. 'There's an animal.' Piglet took Pooh's arm, in case Pooh was frightened. 'Is it one of the Fiercer Animals?' he said, looking the other way. Pooh nodded. 'It's a Jagular,' he said. 'What do Jagulars do?' asked Piglet, hoping that they wouldn't. 'They hide in the branches of trees, and drop on you as you go underneath,' said Pooh. 'Christopher Robin told me.' 'Perhaps we better hadn't go underneath, Pooh. In case he dropped and hurt himself.' 'They don't hurt themselves,' said Pooh. 'They're such very good droppers.'

Piglet still felt that to be underneath a Very Good Dropper would be a mistake, and he was just going to hurry back for something which he had forgotten when the Jagular called out to them. 'Help! Help!' it called. 'That's what Jagulars always do,' said Pooh, much interested. 'They call "Help! Help!" and then when you look up, they drop on you.' 'I'm looking down,' cried Piglet loudly, so as the Jagular shouldn't do the wrong thing by accident. Something very excited next to the Jagular heard him, and squeaked: 'Pooh and Piglet! Pooh and Piglet!' All of sudden Piglet felt that it was a much nicer day than he had thought it was. All warm and sunny—'Pooh!' he cried. 'I believe it's Tigger and Roo!'

19

POOH AND PIGLET GO HUNTING
AND NEARLY CATCH A WOOZLE

The Piglet lived in a very grand house in the middle of a beech-tree, and the beech-tree was in the middle of the forest, and the Piglet lived in the middle of the house. Next to his house was a piece of broken board which had: 'TRESPASSERS W' on it. When Christopher Robin asked the Piglet what it meant, he said it was his grandfather's name, and had been in the family for a long time. Christopher Robin said you couldn't be called Trespassers W, and Piglet said yes, you could, because his grandfather was, and it was short for Trespassers Will, which was short for Trespassers William. And his grandfather had had two names in case he lost one—Trespassers after an uncle, and William after Trespassers.

'I've got two names,' said Christopher Robin carelessly.

'Well, there you are, that proves it,' said Piglet.

One fine winter's day when Piglet was brushing away the snow in front of his house, he happened to look up, and there was Winnie-the-Pooh. Pooh was walking round and round in a circle, thinking of something else, and when Piglet called to him, he just went on walking.

'Hallo!' said Piglet, 'what are you doing?'

'Hunting,' said Pooh.

'Hunting what?'

'Tracking something,' said Winnie-the-Pooh very mysteriously.

'Tracking what?' said Piglet, coming closer

'That's just what I ask myself. I ask myself, "What?"'

'What do you think you'll answer?'

'I shall have to wait until I catch up with it,' said Winnie-the-Pooh. 'Now, look there.' He pointed to the ground in front of him. 'What do you see there?'

'Tracks,' said Piglet. 'Paw-marks.' He gave a little squeak of excitement. 'Oh, Pooh! Do you think it's a—a—a Woozle?'

'It may be,' said Pooh. 'Sometimes it is, and sometimes it isn't. You never can tell with paw-marks.'

With these few words he went on tracking, and Piglet, after watching him for a minute or two, ran after him. Winnie-the-Pooh had come to a sudden stop, and was bending over the tracks in a puzzled sort of way.

'What's the matter?' asked Piglet.

'It's a very funny thing,' said Bear, 'but there seem to be two animals now. This—whatever-it-was—has been joined by another—whatever-it-is—and the two of them are now proceeding in company. Would you mind coming with me, Piglet, in case they turn out to be Hostile Animals?'

Piglet scratched his ear in a nice sort of way, and said that he had nothing to do until Friday, and would be delighted to come, in case it really was a Woozle.

'You mean, in case it really is two Woozles,' said Winnie-the-Pooh, and Piglet said that anyhow he had nothing to do until Friday. So off they went together.

There was a small spinney of larch trees just here, and it seemed as if the two Woozles, if that is what they were, had been going round this spinney; so round this spinney went

Pooh and Piglet after them; Piglet passing the time by telling Pooh what his Grandfather Trespassers W had done to Remove Stiffness after Tracking, and how his Grandfather Trespassers W had suffered in his later years from Shortness of Breath, and other matters of interest, and Pooh wondering what a Grandfather was like, and if perhaps this was Two Grandfathers they were after now, and, if so, whether he would be allowed to take one home and keep it, and what Christopher Robin would say. And still the tracks went on in front of them...

Suddenly Winnie-the-Pooh stopped, and pointed excitedly in front of him. 'Look!'

'What?' said Piglet, with a jump. And then, to show that he hadn't been frightened, he jumped up and down once or twice more in an exercising sort of way.

'The tracks!' said Pooh. 'A third animal has joined the other two!' 'Pooh!' cried Piglet 'Do you think it is another Woozle?'

'No,' said Pooh, 'because it makes different marks. It is either Two Woozles and one, as it might be, Wizzle, or Two, as it might be, Wizzles and one, if so it is, Woozle. Let us continue to follow them.'

So they went on, feeling just a little anxious now, in case the three animals in front of them were of Hostile Intent. And Piglet wished very much that his Grandfather T. W. were there, instead of elsewhere, and Pooh thought how nice it would be if they met Christopher Robin suddenly but quite accidentally, and only because he liked Christopher Robin so much. And then, all of a sudden, Winnie-the-Pooh stopped again, and licked the tip of his nose in a cooling manner, for he was feeling more hot and anxious than ever in his life before. There were four animals in front of them!

'Do you see, Piglet? Look at their tracks! Three, as it were, Woozles, and one, as it was, Wizzle. Another Woozle has joined them!'

And so it seemed to be. There were the tracks; crossing over each other here, getting muddled up with each other there; but, quite plainly every now and then, the tracks of four sets of paws.

'I think,' said Piglet, when he had licked the tip of his nose too, and found that it brought very little comfort, 'I think that I have just remembered something. I have just remembered something that I forgot to do yesterday and sha'n't be able to do to-morrow. So I suppose I really ought to go back and do it now.'

'We'll do it this afternoon, and I'll come with you,' said Pooh.

'It isn't the sort of thing you can do in the afternoon,' said Piglet quickly. 'It's a very particular morning thing, that has to be done in the morning, and, if possible, between the hours of What would you say the time was?'

'About twelve,' said Winnie-the-Pooh, looking at the sun.

'Between, as I was saying, the hours of twelve and twelve five. So, really, dear old Pooh, if you'll excuse me—What's that.'

Pooh looked up at the sky, and then, as he heard the whistle again, he looked up into the branches of a big oak-tree, and then he saw a friend of his.

'It's Christopher Robin,' he said.

'Ah, then you'll be all right,' said Piglet.

'You'll be quite safe with him. Good-bye,' and he trotted off home as quickly as he could, very glad to be Out of All Danger again.

Christopher Robin came slowly down his tree.

'Silly old Bear,' he said, 'what were you doing? First you went round the spinney twice by yourself, and then Piglet ran after you and you went round again together, and then you were just going round a fourth time.'

'Wait a moment,' said Winnie-the-Pooh, holding up his paw.

He sat down and thought, in the most thoughtful way he could think. Then he fitted his paw into one of the Tracks... and then he scratched his nose twice, and stood up.

'Yes,' said Winnie-the-Pooh.

'I see now,' said Winnie-the-Pooh.

'I have been Foolish and Deluded,' said he, 'and I am a Bear of No Brain at All.'

'You're the Best Bear in All the World,' said Christopher Robin soothingly.

'Am I?' said Pooh hopefully. And then he brightened up suddenly.

'Anyhow,' he said, 'it is nearly Luncheon Time.'

So he went home for it.

20

WINNIE-THE-POOH AND SOME BEES

Here is Edward Bear, coming downstairs now, bump, bump, bump, on the back of his head, behind Christopher Robin. It is, as far as he knows, the only way of coming downstairs, but sometimes he feels that there really is another way, if only he could stop bumping for a moment and think of it.

And then he feels that perhaps there isn't. Anyhow, here he is at the bottom, and ready to be introduced to you. Winnie-the-Pooh.

When I first heard his name, I said, just as you are going to say, 'But I thought he was a boy?'

'So did I,' said Christopher Robin.

'Then you can't call him Winnie?'

'I don't.'

'But you said—'

'He's Winnie-the-Pooh. Don't you know what "the" means?'

'Ah, yes, now I do,' I said quickly; and I hope you do too, because it is all the explanation you are going to get.

Sometimes Winnie-the-Pooh likes a game of some sort when he comes downstairs, and sometimes he likes to sit quietly in front of the fire and listen to a story. This evening—

'What about a story?' said Christopher Robin.

'What about a story?' I said.

'Could you very sweetly tell Winnie-the-Pooh one?'

'I suppose I could,' I said. 'What sort of stories does he like?'

'About himself. Because he's that sort of Bear.'

'Oh, I see.'

'So could you very sweetly?'

'I'll try,' I said.

So I tried.

Once upon a time, a very long time ago now, about last Friday, Winnie-the-Pooh lived in a forest all by himself under the name of Sanders.

('What does "under the name" mean?' asked Christopher Robin. 'It means he had the name over the door in gold letters, and lived under it.'

'Winnie-the-Pooh wasn't quite sure,' said Christopher Robin.

'Now I am,' said a growly voice.

'Then I will go on,' said I.)

One day when he was out walking, he came to an open place in the middle of the forest, and in the middle of this place was a large oak-tree, and, from the top of the tree, there came a loud buzzing noise.

Winnie-the-Pooh sat down at the foot of the tree, put his head between his paws and began to think.

First of all he said to himself: 'That buzzing noise means something. You don't get a buzzing noise like that, just buzzing and buzzing, without its meaning something. If there's a buzzing noise, somebody's making a buzzing noise, and the only reason for making a buzzing noise that I know of is because you're a bee.'

Then he thought another long time, and said: 'And the only reason for being a bee that I know of is making honey.'

And then he got up, and said: 'And the only reason for

making honey is so as I can eat it.' So he began to climb the tree.

He climbed and he climbed and he climbed and as he climbed he sang a little song to himself. It went like this:

Isn't it funny

How a bear likes honey?

Buzz! Buzz! Buzz!

I wonder why he does?

Then he climbed a little further... and a little further... and then just a little further. By that time he had thought of another song.

It's a very funny thought that, if Bears were Bees,

They'd build their nests at the bottom of trees.

And that being so (if the Bees were Bears),

We shouldn't have to climb up all these stairs.

He was getting rather tired by this time, so that is why he sang a Complaining Song. He was nearly there now, and if he just stood on that branch...

Crack !

'Oh, help!' said Pooh, as he dropped ten feet on the branch below him.

'If only I hadn't—' he said, as he bounced twenty feet on to the next branch.

'You see, what I meant to do,' he explained, as he turned head-over-heels, and crashed on to another branch thirty feet below, 'what I meant to do—'

'Of course, it was rather—' he admitted, as he slithered very quickly through the next six branches.

'It all comes, I suppose,' he decided, as he said good-bye to the last branch, spun round three times, and flew gracefully into a gorse-bush, 'it all comes of liking honey so much. Oh, help!'

He crawled out of the gorse-bush, brushed the prickles

from his nose, and began to think again. And the first person he thought of was Christopher Robin.

('Was that me?' said Christopher Robin in an awed voice, hardly daring to believe it.

'That was you.'

Christopher Robin said nothing, but his eyes got larger and larger, and his face got pinker and pinker.)

So Winnie-the-Pooh went round to his friend Christopher Robin, who lived behind a green door in another part of the Forest.

'Good morning, Christopher Robin,' he said.

'Good morning, Winnie-the-Pooh,' said you.

'I wonder if you've got such a thing as a balloon about you?'

'A balloon?'

'Yes, I just said to myself coming along: "I wonder if Christopher Robin has such a thing as a balloon about him?" I just said it to myself, thinking of balloons, and wondering.'

'What do you want a balloon for?' you said.

Winnie-the-Pooh looked round to see that nobody was listening, put his paw to his mouth, and said in a deep whisper: 'Honey!'

'But you don't get honey with balloons!'

'I do,' said Pooh.

Well, it just happened that you had been to a party the day before at the house of your friend Piglet, and you had balloons at the party. You had had a big green balloon; and one of Rabbit's relations had had a big blue one, and had left it behind, being really too young to go to a party at all; and so you had brought the green one and the blue one home with you.

'Which one would you like?' you asked Pooh. He put his head between his paws and thought very carefully.

'It's like this,' he said. 'When you go after honey with

a balloon, the great thing is not to let the bees know you're coming. Now, if you have a green balloon, they might think you were only part of the tree, and not notice you, and if you have a blue balloon, they might think you were only part of the sky, and not notice you, and the question is: Which is most likely?'

'Wouldn't they notice you underneath the balloon?' you asked.

'They might or they might not,' said Winnie-the-Pooh. 'You never can tell with bees.' He thought for a moment and said: 'I shall try to look like a small black cloud. That will deceive them.'

'Then you had better have the blue balloon,' you said; and so it was decided.

Well, you both went out with the blue balloon, and you took your gun with you, just in case, as you always did, and Winnie-the-Pooh went to a very muddy place that he knew of, and rolled and rolled until he was black all over; and then, when the balloon was blown up as big as big, and you and Pooh were both holding on to the string, you let go suddenly, and Pooh Bear floated gracefully up into the sky, and stayed there—level with the top of the tree and about twenty feet away from it.

'Hooray!' you shouted.

'Isn't that fine?' shouted Winnie-the-Pooh down to you. 'What do I look like?'

'You look like a Bear holding on to a balloon,' you said.

'Not,' said Pooh anxiously, '—not like a small black cloud in a blue sky?'

'Not very much.'

'Ah, well, perhaps from up here it looks different. And, as I say, you never can tell with bees.'

There was no wind to blow him nearer to the tree, so there he stayed. He could see the honey, he could smell the honey, but he couldn't quite reach the honey.

After a little while he called down to you.

'Christopher Robin!' he said in a loud whisper.

'Hallo!'

'I think the bees suspect something!'

'What sort of thing?'

'I don't know. But something tells me that they're suspicious!'

'Perhaps they think that you're after their honey?'

'It may be that. You never can tell with bees.'

There was another little silence, and then he called down to you again.

'Christopher Robin!'

'Yes?'

'Have you an umbrella in your house?'

'I think so.'

'I wish you would bring it out here, and walk up and down with it, and look up at me every now and then, and say "Tut-tut, it looks like rain." I think, if you did that, it would help the deception which we are practising on these bees.'

Well, you laughed to yourself, 'Silly old Bear!' but you didn't say it aloud because you were so fond of him, and you went home for your umbrella.

'Oh, there you are!' called down Winnie-the-Pooh, as soon as you got back to the tree. 'I was beginning to get anxious. I have discovered that the bees are now definitely suspicious.'

'Shall I put my umbrella up?' you said.

'Yes, but wait a moment. We must be practical. The important bee to deceive is the Queen Bee. Can you see which is the Queen Bee from down there?'

'No.'

'A pity. Well, now, if you walk up and down with your umbrella, saying, "Tut-tut, it looks like rain," I shall do what I can by singing a little Cloud Song, such as a cloud might sing....Go!'

So, while you walked up and down and wondered if it would rain, Winnie-the-Pooh sang this song:

How sweet to be a Cloud
Floating in the Blue!
Every little cloud
Always sings aloud.
'How sweet to be a Cloud
Floating in the Blue!'
It makes him very proud
To be a little cloud.

The bees were still buzzing as suspiciously as ever. Some of them, indeed, left their nests and flew all round the cloud as it began the second verse of this song, and one bee sat down on the nose of the cloud for a moment, and then got up again.

'Christopher—ow!—Robin,' called out the cloud.

'Yes?'

'I have just been thinking, and I have come to a very important decision. These are the wrong sort of bees.'

'Are they?'

'Quite the wrong sort. So I should think they would make the wrong sort of honey, shouldn't you?'

'Would they?'

'Yes. So I think I shall come down.'

'How?' asked you.

Winnie-the-Pooh hadn't thought about this. If he let go of the string, he would fall—bump—and he didn't like the idea of that. So he thought for a long time, and then he said:

'Christopher Robin, you must shoot the balloon with your gun. Have you got your gun?'

'Of course I have,' you said. 'But if I do that, it will spoil the balloon,' you said. 'But if you don't,' said Pooh, 'I shall have to let go, and that would spoil me.'

When he put it like this, you saw how it was, and you aimed very carefully at the balloon, and fired.

'Ow!' said Pooh.

'Did I miss?' you asked.

'You didn't exactly miss,' said Pooh, 'but you missed the balloon.'

'I'm so sorry,' you said, and you fired again, and this time you hit the balloon and the air came slowly out, and Winnie-the-Pooh floated down to the ground.

But his arms were so stiff from holding on to the string of the balloon all that time that they stayed up straight in the air for more than a week, and whenever a fly came and settled on his nose he had to blow it off. And I think—but I am not sure—that that is why he was always called Pooh.

'Is that the end of the story?' asked Christopher Robin.

'That's the end of that one. There are others.'

'About Pooh and Me?'

'And Piglet and Rabbit and all of you. Don't you remember?'

'I do remember, and then when I try to remember, I forget.'

'That day when Pooh and Piglet tried to catch the Heffalump—'

'They didn't catch it, did they?'

'No.'

'Pooh couldn't, because he hasn't any brain. Did I catch it?'

'Well, that comes into the story.'

Christopher Robin nodded.

'I do remember,' he said, 'only Pooh doesn't very well, so that's why he likes having it told to him again. Because then it's a real story and not just a remembering.'

'That's just how I feel,' I said.

Christopher Robin gave a deep sigh, picked his Bear up by the leg, and walked off to the door, trailing Pooh behind him. At the door he turned and said, 'Coming to see me have my bath?' 'I didn't hurt him when I shot him, did I?' 'Not a bit.' He nodded and went out, and in a moment I heard Winnie-the-Pooh—bump, bump, bump—going up the stairs behind him.

21

THE ORDEAL BY WATER

'We will now bathe,' said a voice at the back of my neck. I gave a grunt and went on with my dream. It was a jolly dream, and nobody got up early in it.

'We will now bathe,' repeated Archie.

'Go away,' I said distinctly.

Archie sat down on my knees and put his damp towel on my face.

'When my wife and I took this commodious residence for six weeks,' he said, 'and engaged the sea at great expense to come up to its doors twice a day, it was on the distinct understanding that our guests should plunge into it punctually at seven o'clock every morning.'

'Don't be silly, it's about three now. And I wish you'd get off my knees.'

'It's a quarter-past seven.'

'Then there you are, we've missed it. Well, we must see what we can do for you to-morrow. Good-night.'

Archie pulled all the clothes off me and walked with them to the window.

'Jove, what a day!' he said. 'And can't you smell the sea?'

'I can. Let that suffice. I say, what's happened to my blanket? I must have swallowed it in my sleep.'

'Where's his sponge?' I heard him murmuring to himself as he came away from the window.

'No, no, I'm up,' I shouted, and I sprang out of bed and put on a shirt and a pair of trousers with great speed. 'Where do I take these off again?' I asked. 'I seem to be giving myself a lot of trouble.'

'There is a tent.'

'Won't the ladies want it? Because, if so, I can easily have my bathe later on.'

'The ladies think it's rather too rough to-day.'

'Perhaps they're right,' I said hopefully. 'A woman's instinct—No, I'm NOT a coward.'

It wasn't so bad outside—sun and wind and a blue-and-white sky and plenty of movement on the sea.

'Just the day for a swim,' said Archie cheerily, as he led the way down to the beach.

'I've nothing against the day; it's the hour I object to. The Lancet says you mustn't bathe within an hour of a heavy meal. Well, I'm going to have a very heavy meal within about twenty minutes. That isn't right, you know.'

By the time I was ready the wind had got much colder. I looked out of the tent and shivered.

'Isn't it jolly and fresh?' said Archie, determined to be helpful. 'There are points about the early morning, after all.'

'There are plenty of points about this morning. Where do they get all the sharp stones from? Look at that one there—he's simply waiting for me.'

'You ought to have bought some bathing shoes. I got this pair in the village.'

'Why didn't you tell me so last night?'

'It was too late last night.'

'Well, it's much too early this morning. If you were a gentleman you'd lend me one of yours, and we'd hop down together.'

Archie being no gentleman, he walked and I hobbled to the edge, and there we sat down while he took off his shoes.

'I should like to take this last opportunity,' I said, 'of telling you that up till now I haven't enjoyed this early morning bathe one little bit. I suppose there will be a notable moment when the ecstasy actually begins, but at present I can't see it coming at all. The only thing I look forward to with any pleasure is the telling Dahlia and Myra at breakfast what I think of their cowardice. That and the breakfast itself. Good-bye.'

I got up and waded into the surf.

'One last word,' I said as I looked back at him. 'In my whole career I shall never know a more absolutely beastly and miserable moment than this.' Then a wave knocked me down, and I saw that I had spoken too hastily.

The world may be divided into two classes—those who drink when they swim and those who don't. I am one of the drinkers. For this reason I prefer river bathing to sea bathing.

'It's about time we came out,' I shouted to Archie after the third pint. 'I'm exceeding my allowance.'

'Aren't you glad now you came?' he cried from the top of a wave.

'Very,' I said a moment later from inside it.

But I really did feel glad ten minutes afterwards as I sat on the beach in the sun and smoked a cigarette, and threw pebbles lazily into the sea.

'Holbein, how brave of you!' cried a voice behind me.

'Good-morning. I'm not at all sure that I ought to speak to you.'

'Have you really been taking the sea so early,' said Myra as she sat down between us, 'or did you rumple each other's hair so as to deceive me?'

'I have been taking the sea,' I confessed. 'What you observe out there now is what I left.'

'Oh, but that's what *I* do. That's why I didn't come to-day—because I had so much yesterday.'

'I'm a three-bottle man. I can go on and on and on. And after all these years I have the most sensitive palate of any man living. For instance, I can distinguish between Scarborough and Llandudno quite easily with my eyes shut. Speaking as an expert, I may say that there is nothing to beat a small Cromer and seltzer; though some prefer a Ventnor and dash. Ilfracombe with a slice of lemon is popular, but hardly appeals to the fastidious.'

'Do you know,' said Archie, 'that you are talking drivel? Nobody ought to drivel before breakfast. It isn't decent. What does Dahlia want to do to-day, Myra?'

'Mr. Simpson is coming by the one-thirty.'

'Good; then we'll have a slack day. The strain of meeting Simpson will be sufficient for us. I do hope he comes in a yachting cap—we'll send him back if he doesn't.'

'I told him to bring one,' said Myra. 'I put a P.S. in Dahlia's letter—please bring your telescope and yachting cap. She thought we could have a good day's sailing to-morrow, if you'd kindly arrange about the wind.'

'I'll talk to the crew about it and see what he can do. If we get becalmed we can always throw somebody overboard, of course. Well, I must go in and finish my toilet.'

We got up and climbed slowly back to the house.

'And then,' I said, 'then for the heavy meal.'

22

THE ADVENTURER

Lionel Norwood, from his earliest days, had been marked out for a life of crime. When quite a child he was discovered by his nurse killing flies on the window-pane. This was before the character of the house-fly had become a matter of common talk among scientists, and Lionel (like all great men, a little before his time) had pleaded hygiene in vain. He was smacked hastily and bundled off to a preparatory school, where his aptitude for smuggling sweets would have lost him many a half-holiday had not his services been required at outside-left in the hockey eleven. With some difficulty he managed to pass into Eton, and three years later—with, one would imagine, still more difficulty—managed to get superannuated. At Cambridge he went down-hill rapidly. He would think nothing of smoking a cigar in academical costume, and on at least one occasion he drove a dogcart on Sunday. No wonder that he was requested, early in his second year, to give up his struggle with the Little-go and betake himself back to London.

London is always glad to welcome such people as Lionel Norwood. In no other city is it so simple for a man of easy conscience to earn a living by his wits. If Lionel ever had any scruples (which, after a perusal of the above account of his early days, it may be permitted one to doubt) they were removed by an accident to his solicitor, who was run over in the Argentine on the very day that he arrived there with what was left of Lionel's money. Reduced suddenly to poverty, Norwood had no choice but to enter upon a life of crime.

Except, perhaps, that he used slightly less hair-oil than most, he seemed just the ordinary man about town as he sat in his dressing-gown one fine summer morning and smoked a cigarette. His rooms were furnished quietly and in the best of taste. No signs of his nefarious profession showed themselves to the casual visitor. The appealing letters from the Princess whom he was blackmailing, the wire apparatus which shot the two of spades down his sleeve during the coon-can nights at the club, the thimble and pea with which he had performed the three-card trick so successfully at Epsom last week—all these were hidden away from the common gaze. It was a young gentleman of fashion who lounged in his chair and toyed with a priceless straight-cut.

There was a tap at the door, and Masters, his confidential valet, came in.

'Well,' said Lionel, 'have you looked through the post?'

'Yes, sir,' said the man. 'There's the usual cheque from Her Highness, a request for more time from the lady in Tite Street with twopence to pay on the envelope, and banknotes from the Professor as expected. The young gentleman of Hill Street has gone abroad suddenly, sir.'

'Ah!' said Lionel, with a sudden frown. 'I suppose you'd better cross him off our list, Masters.'

'Yes, sir. I had ventured to do so, sir. I think that's all, except that Mr. Snooks is glad to accept your kind invitation to dinner and bridge to-night. Will you wear the hair-spring coat, sir, or the metal clip?'

Lionel made no answer. He sat plunged in thought. When he spoke it was about another matter.

'Masters,' he said, 'I have found out Lord Fairlie's secret at last. I shall go to see him this afternoon.'

'Yes, sir. Will you wear your revolver, sir, as it's a first call?'

'I think so. If this comes off, Masters, it will make our fortune.'

'I hope so, I'm sure, sir.' Masters placed the whisky within reach and left the room silently.

Alone, Lionel picked up his paper and turned to the Agony Column.

As everybody knows, the Agony Column of a daily paper is not actually so domestic as it seems. When 'Mother' apparently says to 'Floss,' 'Come home at once. Father gone away for week. Bert and Sid longing to see you,' what is really happening is that Barney Hoker is telling Jud Batson to meet him outside the Duke of Westminster's little place at 3 a.m. precisely on Tuesday morning, not forgetting to bring his jemmy and a dark lantern with him. And Floss's announcement next day, 'Coming home with George,' is Jud's way of saying that he will turn up all right, and half thinks of bringing his automatic pistol with him too, in case of accidents.

In this language—which, of course, takes some little learning—Lionel Norwood had long been an expert. The advertisement which he was now reading was unusually elaborate:

'Lost, in a taxi between Baker Street and Shepherd's Bush, a gold-mounted umbrella with initials "J.P." on it. If Ellen will return to her father immediately all will be forgiven. White spot on foreleg. Mother very anxious and desires to return thanks for kind enquiries. Answers to the name of Ponto. *Bis dat qui cito dat.*'

What did it mean? For Lionel it had no secrets. He was reading the revelation by one of his agents of the skeleton in Lord Fairlie's cupboard!

Lord Fairlie was one of the most distinguished members of the Cabinet. His vein of high seriousness, his lofty demeanour, the sincerity of his manner endeared him not only to his own party, but even (astounding as it may seem) to a few high-minded men upon the other side, who admitted, in moments of expansion which they probably regretted afterwards, that he might, after all, be as devoted to his country as they were. For years now his life had been without blemish. It was impossible to believe that even in his youth he could have sown any wild oats; terrible to think that these wild oats might now be coming home to roost.

'What do you require of me?' he said courteously to Lionel, as the latter was shown into his study.

Lionel went to the point at once.

'I am here, my lord,' he said, 'on business. In the course of my ordinary avocations'—the parliamentary atmosphere seemed to be affecting his language—'I ascertained a certain secret in your past life which, if it were revealed, might conceivably have a not undamaging effect upon your career. For my silence in this matter I must demand a sum of fifty thousand pounds.'

Lord Fairlie had grown paler and paler as this speech proceeded.

'What have you discovered?' he whispered. Alas! he knew only too well what the damning answer would be.

'*Twenty years ago,*' said Lionel, '*you wrote a humorous book.*'

Lord Fairlie gave a strangled cry. His keen mind recognized in a flash what a hold this knowledge would give his enemies. *Shafts of Folly*, his book had been called. Already he saw the leading articles of the future:—

'We confess ourselves somewhat at a loss to know whether Lord Fairlie's speech at Plymouth yesterday was intended as a supplement to his earlier work, *Shafts of Folly,* or as a serious offering to a nation impatient of levity in such a crisis....'

'The Cabinet's jester, in whom twenty years ago the country lost an excellent clown without gaining a statesman, was in great form last night....'

'Lord Fairlie has amused us in the past with his clever little parodies; he may amuse us in the future; but as a statesman we can only view him with disgust....'

'Well?' said Lionel at last. 'I think your lordship is wise enough to understand. The discovery of a sense of humour in a man of your eminence—'

But Lord Fairlie was already writing out the cheque.

23

A BREATH OF LIFE

This is the story of a comedy which nearly became a tragedy. In its way it is rather a pathetic story.

The comedy was called The Wooing of Winifred. It was written by an author whose name I forget; produced by the well-known and (as his press-agent has often told us) popular actor-manager, Mr. Levinski; and played by (among others) that very charming young man, Prosper Vane—known locally as Alfred Briggs until he took to the stage. Prosper played the young hero, Dick Seaton, who was actually wooing Winifred. Mr. Levinski himself took the part of a middle-aged man of the world with a slight *embonpoint*; down in the programme as *Sir Geoffrey Throssell* but fortunately still Mr. Levinski. His opening words, as he came on, were, 'Ah, Dick, I have a note for you somewhere,' which gave the audience an interval in which to welcome him, while he felt in all his pockets for the letter. One can bow quite easily while feeling in one's pockets, and it is much more natural than stopping in the middle of an important speech in order to acknowledge any cheers. The realization of this, by a dramatist, is what is called 'stagecraft.' In this case the audience could tell at once that the 'technique' of the author (whose name unfortunately I forget) was going to be all right.

But perhaps I had better describe the whole play as shortly as possible. The theme—as one guessed from the title, even before the curtain rose—was the wooing of Winifred. In the First Act Dick proposed to Winifred and was refused by her, not from lack of love, but for fear lest she might spoil his career, he being one of those big-hearted men with a hip-pocket to whom the open spaces of the world call loudly; whereupon Mr. Levinski took Winifred on one side and told the audience how, when he had been a young man, some good woman had refused him for a similar reason and had been miserable ever since. Accordingly in the Second Act Winifred withdrew her refusal and offered to marry Dick, who declined to take advantage of her offer for fear that she was willing to marry him from pity rather than from love; whereupon Mr. Levinski took Dick on one side and told the audience how, when he had been a young man, he had refused to marry some good woman (a different one) for a similar reason, and had been broken-hearted ever afterwards. In the Third Act it really seemed as though they were coming together at last; for at the beginning of it Mr. Levinski took them both aside and told the audience a parable about a butterfly and a snap-dragon, which was both pretty and helpful, and caused several middle-aged ladies in the first and second rows of the upper circle to say, 'What a nice man Mr. Levinski must be at home, dear!'—the purport of the allegory being to show that both Dick and Winifred were being very silly, as indeed by this time everybody but the author was aware. Unfortunately at that moment a footman entered with a telegram for Miss Winifred, which announced that she had been left fifty thousand pounds by a dead uncle in Australia; and, although Mr. Levinski seized this fresh opportunity to tell the audience how in similar circumstances Pride, to his lasting remorse, had kept him and some good woman (a third one) apart, nevertheless Dick held back once more, for fear lest he should be thought to be marrying her for her money. The curtain comes down as he says, 'Good-bye...good ber-eye.' But there is a Fourth Act, and in the Fourth Act Mr. Levinski has a splendid time. He tells the audience two parables—one about a dahlia and a sheep, which I couldn't quite follow—and three reminiscences of life in India; he brings together finally and for ever these hesitating lovers; and, best of all, he has a magnificent love-scene of his own with a pretty widow, in which we see, for the first time in the play, how love should really be made—not boy-and-girl pretty-pretty love, but the deep emotion felt (and with occasional lapses of memory explained) by a middle-aged man with a slight embonpoint who has knocked about the world a bit and knows life. Mr. Levinski, I need not say, was at his best in this Act.

I met Prosper Vane at the club some ten days before the first night, and asked him how rehearsals were going.

'Oh, all right,' he said. 'But it's a rotten play. I've got such a dashed silly part.'

'From what you told me,' I said, 'it sounded rather good.'

'It's so dashed unnatural. For three whole acts this girl and I are in love with each other, and we know we're in love with each other, and yet we simply fool about. She's a dashed pretty girl, too, my boy. In real life I'd jolly soon—'

'My dear Alfred,' I protested, 'you're not going to fall in love with the girl you have to fall in love with on the stage? I thought actors never did that.'

'They do sometimes; it's a dashed good advertisement. Anyway, it's a silly part, and I'm fed up with it.'

'Yes, but do be reasonable. If Dick got engaged at once to Winifred what would happen to Levinski? He'd have nothing to do.'

Prosper Vane grunted. As he seemed disinclined for further conversation I left him.

The opening night came, and the usual distinguished and fashionable audience (including myself), such as habitually attends Mr. Levinski's first nights, settled down to enjoy itself. Two acts went well. At the end of each Mr. Levinski came before the curtain and bowed to us, and we had the honour of clapping him loud and long. Then the Third Act began....

Now this is how the Third Act ends:—

Exit Sir Geoffrey.

Winifred (breaking the silence): Dick, you heard what he said. Don't let this silly money come between us. I have told you I love you, dear. Won't you—won't you speak to me?

Dick: Winifred, I—(He gets up and walks round the room, his brow knotted, his right fist occasionally striking his left palm. Finally he comes to a stand in front of her.) Winifred, I—(He raises his arms slowly at right angles to his body and lets them fall heavily down again.) I can't. (In a low, hoarse voice) I—can't! (He stands for a moment with bent head; then with a jerk he pulls himself together.) Good-bye! (His hands go out to her, but he draws them back as if frightened to touch her. Nobly) Good ber-eye.

[He squares his shoulders and stands looking at the audience with his chin in the air; then with a shrug of utter despair, which would bring tears into the eyes of any young thing in the pit, he turns and with bent head walks slowly out.]

CURTAIN.

That is how the Third Act ends. I went to the dress rehearsal, and so I know.

How the accident happened I do not know. I suppose Prosper was nervous; I am sure he was very much in love. Anyhow, this is how, on that famous first night, the Third Act ended:—

Exit Sir Geoffrey.

Winifred (breaking the silence): Dick, you heard what he said. Don't let this silly money come between us. I have told you I love you, dear. Won't you—won't you speak to me?

Dick (jumping up): Winifred, I—(with a great gulp) I LOVE YOU!!!

Whereupon he picked her up in his arms and carried her triumphantly off the stage...and after a little natural hesitation the curtain came down.

Behind the scenes all was consternation. Mr. Levinski (absolutely furious) had a hasty consultation with the author (also furious), in the course of which they both saw that the Fourth Act as written was now an impossibility. Poor Prosper, who had almost immediately recovered his sanity, tremblingly suggested that Mr. Levinski should announce that, owing to the sudden illness of Mr. Vane, the Fourth Act could not be given. Mr. Levinski was kind enough to consider this suggestion not entirely stupid; his own idea having been (very regretfully) to leave out the two parables and three reminiscences from India and concentrate on the love-scene with the widow.

'Yes, yes,' he said. 'Your plan is better. I will say you are ill. It is true; you are mad. To-morrow we will play it as it was written.'

'You can't,' said the author gloomily. 'The critics won't come till the Fourth Act, and they'll assume that the Third Act ended as it did to-night. The Fourth Act will seem all nonsense to them.'

'True. And I was so good, so much myself, in that Act.' He turned to Prosper. 'You—fool!'

'Or there's another way,' began the author. 'We might—'

And then a gentleman in the gallery settled it from the front of the curtain. There was nothing in the programme to show that the play was in four acts. 'The Time is the present day and the Scene is in Sir Geoffrey Throssell's town-house,' was all it said. And the gentleman in the gallery, thinking it was all over, and being pleased with the play and particularly with the realism of the last moment of it, shouted *'Author!'* And suddenly everybody else cried 'Author! Author!' The play was ended.

I said that this was the story of a comedy which nearly became a tragedy. But it turned out to be no tragedy at all. In the three acts to which Prosper Vane had condemned it the play appealed to both critics and public; for the Fourth Act (as he recognised so clearly) was unnecessary, and would have spoilt the balance of it entirely. Best of all, the shortening of the play demanded that some entertainment should be provided in front of it, and this enabled Mr. Levinski to introduce to the public Professor Wollabollacolla and Princess Collabollawolla, the famous exponents of the Bongo-Bongo, that fascinating Central African war dance which was soon to be the rage of society. But though, as a result, the takings of the Box Office surpassed all Mr. Levinski's previous records, our friend Prosper Vane received no practical acknowledgment of his services. He had to be content with the hand and heart of the lady who played Winifred, and the fact that Mr. Levinski was good enough to attend the wedding. There was, in fact, a photograph in all the papers of Mr. Levinski doing it.

24

CHUM

It is Chum's birthday to-morrow and I am going to buy him a little whip for a present, with a whistle at the end of it. When I next go into the country to see him I shall take it with me and explain it to him. Two day's firmness would make him quite a sensible dog. I have often threatened to begin the treatment on my very next visit, but somehow it has been put off; the occasion of his birthday offers a last opportunity.

It is rather absurd, though, to talk of birthdays in connection with Chum, for he has been no more than three months old since we have had him. He is a black spaniel who has never grown up. He has a beautiful astrachan coat which gleams when the sun is on it; but he stands so low in the water that the front of it is always getting dirty, and his ears and the ends of his trousers trail in the mud. A great authority has told us that, but for three white hairs on his shirt (upon so little do class distinctions hang), he would be a Cocker of irreproachable birth. A still greater authority has sworn that he is a Sussex. The family is indifferent—it only calls him a Silly Ass. Why he was christened Chum I do not know; and as he never recognises the name it does not matter.

When he first came to stay with us I took him a walk round the village. I wanted to show him the lie of the land.

He had never seen the country before and was full of interest. He trotted into a cottage garden and came back with something to show me.

'You'll never guess,' he said. 'Look!' and he dropped at my feet a chick just out of the egg.

I smacked his head and took him into the cottage to explain.

'My dog,' I said, 'has eaten one of your chickens.'

Chum nudged me in the ankle and grinned.

'Two of your chickens,' I corrected myself, looking at the fresh evidence which he had just brought to light.

'You don't want me any more?' said Chum, as the financial arrangements proceeded. 'Then I'll just go and find somewhere for these two.'

And he picked them up and trotted into the sun.

When I came out I was greeted effusively.

'This is a wonderful day,' he panted, as he wriggled his body. 'I didn't know the country was like this. What do we do now?'

'We go home,' I said, and we went.

That was Chum's last day of freedom. He keeps inside the front gate now. But he is still a happy dog; there is plenty doing in the garden. There are beds to walk over, there are blackbirds in the apple-tree to bark at. The world is still full of wonderful things. 'Why only last Wednesday,' he will tell you, 'the fishmonger left his basket in the drive. There was a haddock in it, if you'll believe me, for Master's breakfast, so of course I saved it for him. I put it on the grass just in front of his study window, where he'd be *sure* to notice it. Bless you, there's always *something* to do in this house. One is never idle.'

And even when there is nothing doing he is still happy, waiting cheerfully upon events until they arrange themselves for his amusement. He will sit for twenty minutes opposite the garden bank, watching for a bumble bee to come out of its hole. 'I saw him go in,' he says to himself, 'so he's bound to come out. Extraordinary interesting world.' But to his inferiors (such as the gardener) he pretends that it is not pleasure but duty which keeps him. 'Don't talk to me, fool. Can't you see that I've got a job on here?'

Chum has found, however, that his particular mission in life is to purge his master's garden of all birds. This keeps him busy. As soon as he sees a blackbird on the lawn he is in full cry after it. When he gets to the place and finds the blackbird gone he pretends that he was going there anyhow; he gallops round in circles, rolls over once or twice, and then trots back again. 'You didn't *really* think I was such a fool as to try to catch a *blackbird*?' he says to us. 'No, I was just taking a little run—splendid thing for the figure.'

And it is just Chum's little runs over the beds which call aloud for firmness—which, in fact, have inspired my birthday present to him. But there is this difficulty to overcome first. When he came to live with us, an arrangement was entered into (so he says) by which one bed was given to him as his own. In that bed he could wander at will, burying bones and biscuits, hunting birds. This may have been so, but it is a pity that nobody but Chum knows definitely which is the bed.

'Chum, you bounder,' I shout, as he is about to wade through the herbaceous border.

He takes no notice; he struggles through to the other side. But a sudden thought strikes him, and he pushes his way back again.

'Did you call me?' he says.

'How dare you walk over the flowers?'

He comes up meekly.

'I suppose I've done something wrong,' he says, 'but I can't think what.'

I smack his head for him. He waits until he is quite sure I

have finished and then jumps up with a bark, wipes his paws on my trousers and trots into the herbaceous border again.

'Chum!' I cry.

He sits down in it and looks all round him in amazement.

'My own bed!' he murmurs. 'Given to me!'

I don't know what it is in him which so catches hold of you. His way of sitting, a reproachful statue, motionless outside the window of whomever he wants to come out and play with him—until you can bear it no longer, but must either go into the garden or draw down the blinds for one day; his habit when you *are* out, of sitting up on his back legs and begging you with his front paws to come and *do* something—a trick entirely of his own invention, for no one would think of teaching him anything; his funny nautical roll when he walks, which is nearly a swagger, and gives him always the air of having just come back from some rather dashing adventure; beyond all this there is still something. And whatever it is, it is something, which every now and then compels you to bend down and catch hold of his long silky ears, to look into his honest eyes and say—

'You silly old ass! You dear old silly old ass!'

25

COMMON

Seated in your comfortable club, my very dear sir, or in your delightful drawing-room, madam, you may smile pityingly at the idea of a mascot saving anybody's life. 'What will be, will be,' you say to yourself (or in Italian to your friends), 'and to suppose that a charm round the neck of a soldier will divert a German shell is ridiculous.' But out there, through the crumps, things look otherwise.

Common had sat on the mantelpiece at home. An ugly little ginger dog, with a bit of red tape for his tongue and two black beads for his eyes, he viewed his limited world with an air of innocent impertinence very attractive to visitors. Common he looked and Common he was called, with a Christian name of Howard for registration. For six months he sat there, and no doubt he thought that he had seen all that there was to see of the world when the summons came which was to give him so different an outlook on life.

For that summons meant the breaking up of his home. Master was going wandering from trench to trench, Mistress from one person's house to another person's house. She no doubt would take Common with her; or perhaps she couldn't be bothered with an ugly little ginger dog, and he would be stored in some repository, boarded out in some Olympic kennel.

'Or do you *possibly* think Master might—'

He looked very wistful that last morning, so wistful that Mistress couldn't bear it, and she slipped him in hastily between the revolver and the boracic powder, 'Just to look after you,' she said. So Common came with me to France.

His first view of the country was at Rouen, when he sat at the entrance to my tent and hooshed the early morning flies away. His next at a village behind the lines, where he met stout fellows of 'D' Company and took the centre of the table at mess in the apple orchard; and moreover was introduced to a French maiden of two, with whom, at the instigation of the seconds in the business—her mother and myself—a prolonged but monotonous conversation in the French tongue ensued, Common, under suitable pressure, barking idiomatically, and the maiden, carefully prompted, replying with the native for 'Bow-wow.' A pretty greenwood scene beneath the apple-trees, and in any decent civilization the great adventure would have ended there. But Common knew that it was not only for this that he had been brought out, and that there was more arduous work to come.

Once more he retired to the valise, for we were making now for a vill—for a heap of bricks near the river; you may guess the river. It was about this time that I made a little rhyme for him:

There was a young puppy called Howard,
Who at fighting was rather a coward;
He never quite ran
When the battle began,
But he started at once to bow-wow hard.

A good poet is supposed to be superior to the exigencies of rhyme, but I am afraid that in any case Common's reputation had to be sacrificed to them. To be lyrical over anybody called

Howard Common without hinting that he—well, try for yourself. Anyhow it was a lie, as so much good poetry is.

There came a time when valises were left behind and life for a fortnight had to be sustained on a pack. One seems to want very many things, but there was no hesitation about Common's right to a place. So he came to see his first German dug-out, and to get a proper understanding of this dead bleached land and the great work which awaited him there. It was to blow away shells and bullets when they came too near the master in whose pocket he sat.

In this he was successful; but I think that the feat in which he takes most pride was performed one very early summer morning. A telephone line had to be laid, and, for reasons obvious to Common, rather rapidly. It was laid safely—a mere nothing to him by this time. But when it was joined up to the telephone in the front line, then he realized that he was called upon to be not only a personal mascot, but a mascot to the battalion, and he sat himself upon the telephone and called down a blessing on that cable, so that it remained whole for two days and a night when by all the rules it should have been in a thousand pieces. 'And even if I didn't *really* do it all myself,' he said, 'anyhow I *did* make some of the men in the trench smile a little that morning, and there wasn't so *very* much smiling going on just then, you know.'

After that morning he lived in my pocket, sometimes sniffing at an empty pipe, sometimes trying to read letters from Mistress which joined him every day. We had gone North to a more gentlemanly part of the line, and his duties took but little of his time, so that anything novel, like a pair of pliers or an order from the Director of Army Signals, was always welcome. To begin with he took up rather more than his fair share of the pocket, but he rapidly thinned down. Alas! in the rigours of the campaign he also lost his voice; and his little black collar, his only kit, disappeared.

Then, just when we seemed settled for the winter, we were ordered South again. Common knew what that meant, a busy time for him. We moved down slowly, and he sampled billet after billet, but we arrived at last and sat down to wait for the day.

And then he began to get nervous. Always he was present when the operations were discussed; he had seen all the maps; he knew exactly what was expected of us. And he didn't like it.

'It's more than a fellow can do,' he said; 'at least to be certain of. I can blow away the shells in front and the shells from the right, but if Master's map is correct we're going to get enfiladed from the left as well, and one can't be *everywhere*. This wants thinking about.'

So he dived head downwards into the deepest recesses of my pocket and abandoned himself to thought. A little later he came up with a smile...

Next morning I stayed in bed and the doctor came. Common looked over his shoulder as he read the thermometer.

'A hundred and four,' said Common. 'Golly! I hope I haven't over-done it.'

He came with me to the clearing station.

'I only just blowed a germ at him,' he said wistfully—'one I found in his pocket. I only just blowed it at him.'

We went down to the base hospital together; we went back to England. And in the hospital in England Common suddenly saw his mistress again.

'I've brought him back, Missis,' he said. 'Here he is. Have I done well?'

◆

He sits now in a little basket lined with flannel, a hero returned from the War. Round his neck he wears the regimental colours, and on his chest will be sewn whatever medal is given to those who have served faithfully on the Western Front. Seated in your comfortable club, my very dear sir, or in your delightful drawing-room, madam, you smile pityingly...

Or perhaps you don't.

26

DEFINITIONS

As soon as we had joined the ladies after dinner Gerald took up a position in front of the fire.

'Now that the long winter evenings are upon us,' he began—

'Anyhow, it's always dark at half-past nine,' said Norah.

'Not in the morning,' said Dennis, who has to be excused for anything foolish he says since he became obsessed with golf.

'Please don't interrupt,' I begged. 'Gerald is making a speech.'

'I was only going to say that we might have a little game of some sort. Norah, what's the latest parlour game from London?'

'Tell your uncle,' I urged, 'how you amuse yourselves at the Lyceum.'

'Do you know "Hunt the Pencil"?'

'No. What do you do?'

'You collect five pencils; when you've got them, I'll tell you another game.'

'Bother these pencil games,' said Dennis, taking an imaginary swing with a paper-knife. 'I hope it isn't too brainy.'

'You'll want to know how to spell,' said Norah severely, and she went to the writing-desk for some paper.

In a little while—say, half an hour—we had each a sheet of paper and a pencil, and Norah was ready to explain.

'It's called Definitions. I expect you all know it.'

We assured her we didn't.

'Well, you begin by writing down five or six letters, one underneath the other. We might each suggest one. "E."'

We weighed in with ours, and the result was E P A D U.

'Now you write them backwards.'

There was a moment's consternation.

'Like "bath-mat"?' said Dennis. 'An "e" backwards looks so silly.'

'Stupid—like this,' explained Norah. She showed us her paper.

E	U
P	D
A	A
D	P
U	E

'This is thrilling,' said Mrs. Gerald, pencilling hard.

'Then everybody has to fill in words all the way down, your first word beginning with "e" and ending with "u," and so on. See?'

Gerald leant over Dennis and explained carefully to him, and in a little while we all saw.

'Then, when everybody's finished, we define our words in turn, and the person who guesses a word first gets a mark. That's all.'

'And a very good game too,' I said, and I rubbed my head and began to think.

'Of course,' said Norah, after a quarter of an hour's silence, 'you want to make the words difficult and define them as subtly as possible.'

'Of course,' I said, wrestling with 'E—U.' I could only think of one word, and it was the one everybody else was certain to have.

'Are we all ready? Then somebody begin.'

'You'd better begin, Norah, as you know the game,' said Mrs. Gerald.

We prepared to begin.

'Mine,' said Norah, 'is a bird.'

'Emu,' we all shouted; but I swear I was first.

'Yes.'

'I don't think that's a very subtle definition,' said Dennis. 'You promised to be as subtle as possible.'

'Go on, dear,' said Gerald to his wife.

'Well, this is rather awkward. Mine is—'

'Emu,' I suggested.

'You must wait till she has defined it,' said Norah sternly.

'Mine is a sort of feathered animal.'

'Emu,' I said again. In fact, we all said it.

Gerald coughed. 'Mine,' he said, 'isn't exactly a—fish, because it—'

'Emu,' said everybody.

'That was subtler,' said Dennis, 'but it didn't deceive us.'

'Your turn,' said Norah to me. And they all leant forward ready to say 'Emu.'

'Mine,' I said, 'is—all right, Dennis, you needn't look so excited—is a word I once heard a man say at the Zoo.'

There was a shriek of 'Emu!'

'Wrong,' I said.

Everybody was silent.

'Where did he say it?' asked Norah at last. 'What was he doing?'

'He was standing outside the Emu's cage.'

'It must have been Emu.'

'It wasn't.'

'Perhaps there's another animal beginning with "e" and ending with "u,"' suggested Dennis. 'He might have said, "Look here, I'm tired of this old Emu, let's go and see the E-doesn't-mu," or whatever it's called.'

'We shall have to give it up,' said Norah at last. 'What is it?'

'Ebu,' I announced. 'My man had a bad cold, and he said, "Look, Baria, there's ad Ebu." Er—what do I get for that?'

'Nothing,' said Norah coldly. 'It isn't fair. Now, Mr. Dennis.'

'Mine is *not* Emu, and it couldn't be mistaken for Emu; not even if you had a sore throat and a sprained ankle. And it has nothing to do with the Zoo, and—'

'Well, what is it?'

'It's what you say at golf when you miss a short putt.'

'I doubt it,' I said.

'Not what Gerald says,' said his wife.

'Well, it's what you might say. What Horace would have said.'

'"Eheu"—good,' said Gerald, while his wife was asking 'Horace who?'

We moved on to the next word, P—D.

'Mine,' said Norah, 'is what you might do to a man whom you didn't like, but it's a delightful thing to have and at the same time you would hate to be in it.'

'Are you sure you know what you are talking about, dear?' said Mrs. Gerald gently.

'Quite,' said Norah with the confidence of extreme youth.

'Could you say it again very slowly,' asked Dennis, 'indicating by changes in the voice which character is speaking?'

She said it again.

'"Pound,"' said Gerald. 'Good—one to me.'

Mrs. Gerald had 'pod,' Gerald had 'pond'; but they didn't define them very cleverly and they were soon guessed. Mine, unfortunately, was also guessed at once.

'It is what Dennis's golf is,' I said.

'"Putrid,"' said Gerald correctly.

'Mine,' said Dennis, 'is what everybody has two of.'

'Then it's not "pound,"' I said, 'because I've only got one and ninepence.'

'At least, it's best to have two. Sometimes you lose one. They're very useful at golf. In fact, absolutely necessary.'

'Have you got two?'

'Yes.'

I looked at Dennis's enormous hands spread out on his knees.

'Is it "pud"?' I asked. 'It is? Are those the two? Good heavens!' and I gave myself a mark.

A—A was the next, and we had the old Emu trouble.

'Mine,' said Norah—'mine is rather a meaningless word.'

'"Abracadabra,"' shouted everybody.

'Mine,' said Miss Gerald, 'is a very strange word, which—'

'"Abracadabra,"' shouted everybody.

'Mine,' said Gerald, 'is a word which used to be—'

'"Abracadabra,"' shouted everybody.

'Mine,' I said to save trouble, 'is "Abracadabra."'

'Mine,' said Dennis, 'isn't. It's what you say at golf when—'

'Oh lor!' I groaned. 'Not again.'

'When you hole a long putt for a half.'

'You generally say, "What about *that* for a good putt, old thing? Thirty yards at least,"' suggested Gerald.

'No.'

'Is it—is it "Alleluia"?' suggested Mrs. Gerald timidly.

'Yes.'

'Dennis,' I said, 'you're an ass.'

'And now,' said Norah at the end of the game, 'who's won?'

They counted up their marks.

'Ten,' said Norah.

'Fifteen,' said Gerald.

'Three,' said his wife.

'Fourteen,' said Dennis.

They looked at me.

'I'm afraid I forgot to put all mine down,' I said, 'but I can easily work it out. There were five words, and five definitions of each word. Twenty-five marks to be gained altogether. You four have got—er—let's see—forty-two between you. That leaves me—'

'That leaves you *minus* seventeen,' said Dennis. 'I'm afraid you've lost, old man.' He took up the shovel and practised a few approach shots. 'It's rather a good game.'

I think so too. It's a good game, but, like all paper games, its scoring wants watching.

27

GETTING THE NEEDLE

He was a pale, enthusiastic young man of the name of Simms; and he held forth to us at great length about his latest hobby.

'Now I'll just show you a little experiment,' he wound up, 'one that I have never known to fail. First of all I want you to hide a needle somewhere, while I am out of the room. You must stick it where it can be seen—on a chair—or on the floor if you like. Then I shall come back blindfolded and find it.'

'Oh, Mr. Simms!' we all said.

'Now, which one of you has the strongest will?'

We pushed Jack forward. Jack is at any rate a big man.

'Very well. I shall want you to take my hand when I come in, and look steadily at the needle—concentrate all your thoughts on it. I, on the other hand, shall make my mind a perfect blank. Then your thoughts will gradually pass into my brain, and I shall feel myself as it were, dragged in the direction of the needle.'

'And I shall feel myself, as it were, dragged after you?' said Jack.

'Yes; you mustn't put any strain on my arm at all. Let me go just where I like, only will me to go in the right direction. Now then.'

He took out his handkerchief, put it hastily back, and said: 'First I shall want to borrow a handkerchief or something.'

Well, we blindfolded him, and led him out of the room. Then Muriel got a needle, which, after some discussion, was stuck into the back of the Chesterfield. Simms returned and took Jack's left hand.

They stood there together, Jack frowning earnestly at the needle, and Simms swaying uncertainly at the knees. Suddenly his knees went in altogether, and he made a little zig-zag dash across the room, as though he were taking cover. Jack lumbered after him, instinctively bending his head, too. They were brought up by the piano, which Simms struck with great force. We all laughed, and Jack apologised.

'You told me to let you go where you liked, you know,' he said.

'Yes, yes,' said Simms rather peevishly, 'but you should have willed me not to hit the piano.'

As he spoke he tripped over a small stool and, flinging out an arm to save himself, swept two photograph frames off an occasional table.

'By Jove,' said Jack, 'that's jolly good. I saw you were going to do that, and I willed that the flower vase should be spared. I'm getting on.'

'I think you had better start from the door again,' I suggested. 'Then you can get a clear run.'

They took up their original positions.

'You must think hard, please,' said Simms again. 'My mind is a perfect blank, and yet I can feel nothing coming.'

Jack made terrible faces at the needle. Then, without warning, Simms flopped on to the floor at full length, pulling Jack after him.

'You mustn't mind if I do that,' he said, getting up slowly.

'No,' said Jack, dusting himself.

'I felt irresistibly compelled to go down,' said Simms.

'So did I,' said Jack.

'The needle is very often hidden in the floor, you see. You are sure you are looking at it?'

They were in a corner with their back to it; and Jack, after trying in vain to get it over his right shoulder or his left, bent down and focussed it between his legs. This must have connected the current; for Simms turned right round and marched up to the needle.

'There!' he said triumphantly, taking off the bandage.

We all clapped, while Jack poured himself out a whisky. Simms turned to him.

'You have a very strong will indeed,' he said, 'one of the strongest I have met. Now, would one of the ladies like to try?'

'Oh, I'm sure I couldn't,' said all the ladies.

'I should like to do it again,' said Simms modestly. 'Perhaps you, Sir?'

'All right, I'll try,' I said.

When Simms was outside I told them my idea.

'I'll hold the needle in my other hand,' I said, 'and then I can always look at it easily, and it will always be in a different place, which ought to muddle him.'

We fetched him in, and he took my left hand...

'No, it's no good,' he said at last. 'I don't seem to get it. Let me try the other hand.'

I had no time to warn him. He clasped the other hand firmly; and from the shriek that followed it seemed that he got it. There ensued the 'perfect blank' that he had insisted on all the evening. Then he pulled off the bandage, and showed a very angry face.

Well, we explained how accidental it was, and begged him to try again. He refused rather sulkily.

Suddenly Jack said: 'I believe I could do it blindfolded. Miss

Muriel, will you look at the needle, and see if you can will me?'

Simms bucked up a bit, and seemed keen on the idea. So Jack was blindfolded, the needle hid, and Muriel took his hand.

'Now is your mind a perfect blank?' said Simms to Jack.

'It always is,' said Jack.

'Very well then. You ought soon to feel in a dreamy state, as though you were in another world. Miss Muriel, you must think only of the needle.'

Jack held her hand tight, and looked most idiotically peaceful. After three minutes Simms spoke again.

'Well?' he said, eagerly.

'I've got the dreamy, other-world state perfectly,' said Jack, and then he gave at the knees, just for the look of the thing.

'This is silly,' said Muriel, trying to get her hand away.

Jack staggered violently, and gripped her hand again.

'Please, Miss Muriel,' implored Simms. 'I feel sure he is just going to do it.'

Jack staggered again, sawed the air with his disengaged hand, and then turned right round and marched for the door, dragging Muriel behind him. The door slammed after them.

There is a little trick of sitting on a chair and picking a pin out of it with the teeth. I started Simms—who was all eagerness to follow the pair, and find out the mysterious force that was drawing them—upon this trick, for Jack is one of my best friends. When Jack and Muriel came back from the billiard-room and announced that they were engaged, Simms was on his back on the floor with the chair on the top of him—explaining, for the fourth time, that if the thing had not overbalanced at the critical moment he would have secured the object. There is much to be said for this view.

28

THE HANDICAP OF SEX

I found myself in the same drawing-room with Anne the other day, so I offered her one of my favourite sandwiches. (I hadn't seen her for some time, and there were plenty in the plate.)

'If you are coming to talk to me,' she said, 'I think I had better warn you that I am a Bolshevist.'

'Then you won't want a sandwich,' I said gladly, and I withdrew the plate.

'I suppose,' said Anne, 'that what I really want is a vote.'

'Haven't you got one? Sorry; I mean, of course you haven't got one.'

'But it isn't only that. I want to see the whole position of women altered. I want to see—'

I looked round for her mother.

'Tell me,' I said gently; 'when did this come over you?'

'In the last few weeks,' said Anne. 'And I don't wonder.'

I settled down with the sandwiches to listen.

Anne first noted symptoms of it at a luncheon-party at the beginning of the month. She had asked the young man on her right if she could have some of his salt, and as he passed it to her he covered up any embarrassment she might be feeling by saying genially, 'Well, and how long is this coal strike going to last?'

'I don't know,' said Anne truthfully.

'I suppose you're ready for the Revolution? The billiard-room and all the spare bedrooms well stocked?'

Anne saw that this was meant humorously, and she laughed.

'I expect we shall be all right,' she said.

'You'll have to give a coal-party, and invite all your friends. "Fire, 9—12."'

'What a lovely idea!' said Anne, smiling from sheer habit. 'Mind you come.' She got her face straight again with a jerk and turned to the solemn old gentleman on her other side.

He was ready for her.

'This is a terrible disaster for the country, this coal strike,' he said.

'Isn't it?' said Anne; and feeling that that was inadequate, added, 'Terrible!'

'I don't know what's happening to the country.'

Anne crumbled her bread, and having reviewed a succession of possible replies, each more fatuous than the last, decided to remain silent.

'Everything will be at a standstill directly,' her companion went on. 'Already trade is leaving the country. America—'

'I suppose so,' said Anne gloomily.

'Once stop the supplies of coal, you see, and you drain the life-blood of the country.'

'Of course,' said Anne, and looked very serious.

After lunch an extremely brisk little man took her in hand.

'Have you been studying this coal strike question at all?' he began.

'I read the papers,' said Anne.

'Ah, but you don't get it there. They don't tell you—they don't tell you. Now I know a man who is actually *in* it, and he *says*—and he knows this for a fact—that from the moment when the *first man* downed tools—from the very moment when he downed tools...'

Anne edged away from him nervously. Her face had assumed an expression of wild interest which she was certain couldn't last much longer.

'Now, take coal at the pit's mouth,' he went on—'at the *pit's mouth*'—he shook a forefinger at her—'at the pit's mouth—and I know this for a *fact*—the *royalties*, the royalties are—'

'It's awful,' said Anne. 'I *know*.'

She went home feeling a little disturbed. There was something in her mind, a dim sense of foreboding, which kept casting its shadow across her pleasanter thoughts; 'Just as you feel,' she said, 'when you *know* you've got to go to the dentist.' But they had a big dinner-party that evening, and Anne, full of the joy of life, was not going to let anything stand in the way of her enjoyment of it.

Her man began on the stairs.

'Well,' he said, 'what about the coal strike? When are you going to start your coal-parties? "Fire, 10—2." They say that that's going to be the new rage.' He smiled reassuringly at her. He was giving the impression that he *could* have been very, very serious over this terrible business, but that for her sake he was wearing the mask. In the presence of women a man must make light of danger.

Anne understood then what was troubling her; and as, half-way through dinner, the man on her other side turned to talk to her, she shot an urgent question at him. At any cost she must know the worst.

'*How* long will the strike last?' she said earnestly. 'That's just what I was going to ask you,' he said. 'I fear it may be months.'

Anne sighed deeply.

I took the last sandwich and put down the plate.

'And that,' said Anne, 'was three weeks ago.'

'It has been the same ever since?' I asked, beginning on a new plate.

'Every day. I'm tired of it. I shrink from every new man I meet. I wait nervously for the word "coal," feeling that I shall scream when it comes. Oh, I want a vote or something. I don't know what I want, but I *hate* men! Why should they think that everything they say to us is funny or clever or important? Why should they talk to us as if we were children? Why should they take it for granted that it's our duty to *listen* always?'

I rose with dignity. Dash it all, who had been doing the listening for the last half-hour?

'You are run down,' I said. 'What you want is a tonic.'

Quite between ourselves, though, I really think—

But no. We men must stick together.

29

THE LUCKY MONTH

'Know thyself,' said the old Greek motto. (In Greek—but this is an English book.) So I bought a little red volume called, tersely enough, *Were you born in January?* I was; and, reassured on this point, the author told me all about myself.

For the most part he told me nothing new. 'You are,' he said in effect, 'good-tempered, courageous, ambitious, loyal, quick to resent wrong, an excellent *raconteur*, and a leader of men.' True. 'Generous to a fault'—(Yes, I was overdoing that rather)—'you have a ready sympathy with the distressed. People born in this month will always keep their promises.' And so on. There was no doubt that the author had the idea all right. Even when he went on to warn me of my weaknesses he maintained the correct note. 'People born in January,' he said, 'must be on their guard against working too strenuously. Their extraordinarily active brains—' Well, you see what he means. It *is* a fault perhaps, and I shall be more careful in future. Mind, I do not take offence with him for calling my attention to it. In fact, my only objection to the book is its surface application to *all* the people who were born in January. There should have been more distinction made between me and the rabble.

I have said that he told me little that was new. In one matter, however, he did open my eyes. He introduced me to an aspect of myself entirely unsuspected.

'They,' he said—meaning me, 'have unusual business capacity, and are destined to be leaders in great commercial enterprises.'

One gets at times these flashes of self-revelation. In an instant I realised how wasted my life had been; in an instant I resolved that here and now I would put my great gifts to their proper uses. I would be a leader in an immense commercial enterprise.

One cannot start commercial enterprises without capital. The first thing was to determine the exact nature of my balance at the bank. This was a matter for the bank to arrange, and I drove there rapidly.

'Good morning,' I said to the cashier, 'I am in rather a hurry. May I have my pass-book?'

He assented and retired. After an interminable wait, during which many psychological moments for commercial enterprise must have lapsed, he returned.

'I think *you* have it,' he said shortly.

'Thank you,' I replied, and drove rapidly home again.

A lengthy search followed; but after an hour of it one of those white-hot flashes of thought, such as only occur to the natural business genius, seared my mind and sent me post-haste to the bank again.

'After all,' I said to the cashier, 'I only want to know my balance. What is it?'

He withdrew and gave himself up to calculation. I paced the floor impatiently. Opportunities were slipping by. At last he pushed a slip of paper across at me. My balance!

It was in four figures. Unfortunately two of them were shillings and pence. Still, there was a matter of fifty pounds odd as well, and fortunes have been built up on less.

Out in the street I had a moment's pause. Hitherto I had

regarded my commercial enterprise in the bulk, as a finished monument of industry; the little niggling preliminary details had not come up for consideration. Just for a second I wondered how to begin.

Only for a second. An unsuspected talent which has long lain dormant needs, when waked, a second or so to turn round in. At the end of that time I had made up my mind. I knew exactly what I would do. I would ring up my solicitor.

'Hallo, is that you? Yes, this is me. What? Yes, awfully, thanks. How are you? Good. Look here, come and lunch with me. What? No, at once. Good-bye.'

Business, particularly that sort of commercial enterprise to which I had now decided to lend my genius, can only be discussed properly over a cigar. During the meal itself my solicitor and I indulged in the ordinary small-talk of the pleasure-loving world.

'You're looking very fit,' said my solicitor. 'No, not fat, *fit.*'

'You don't think I'm looking thin?' I asked anxiously. 'People are warning me that I may be overdoing it rather. They tell me that I must be seriously on my guard against brain strain.'

'I suppose they think you oughtn't to strain it too suddenly,' said my solicitor. Though he is now a solicitor he was once just an ordinary boy like the rest of us, and it was in those days that he acquired the habit of being rude to me, a habit he has never quite forgotten.

'What is an onyx?' I said, changing the conversation.

'Why?' asked my solicitor, with his usual business acumen.

'Well, I was practically certain that I had seen one in the Zoo, in the reptile house, but I have just learnt that it is my lucky month stone. Naturally I want to get one.'

The coffee came and we settled down to commerce.

'I was just going to ask you,' said my solicitor—'have you any money lying idle at the bank? Because if so—'

'Whatever else it is doing, it isn't lying idle,' I protested. 'I was at the bank to-day, and there were men chivying it about with shovels all the time.'

'Well, how much have you got?'

'About fifty pounds.'

'It ought to be more than that.'

'That's what I say, but you know what those banks are. Actual merit counts for nothing with them.'

'Well, what did you want to do with it?'

'Exactly. That was why I rang you up. I—er—' This was really my moment, but somehow I was not quite ready to seize it. My vast commercial enterprise still lacked a few trifling details. 'Er—I—well, it's like that.'

'I might get you a few ground rents.'

'Don't. I shouldn't know where to put them.'

'But if you really have fifty pounds simply lying idle I wish you'd lend it to me for a bit. I'm confoundedly hard up.'

('*Generous to a fault, you have a ready sympathy with the distressed.*' Dash it, what could I do?)

'Is it quite etiquette for clients to lend solicitors money?' I asked. 'I thought it was always solicitors who had to lend it to clients. If I must, I'd rather lend it to you—I mean I'd dislike it less—as to the old friend of my childhood.'

'Yes, that's how I wanted to pay it back.'

'Bother. Then I'll send you a cheque to-night,' I sighed.

And that's where we are at the moment. 'People born in this month always keep their promises.' The money has got to go to-night. If I hadn't been born in January, I shouldn't be sending it; I certainly shouldn't have promised it; I shouldn't even have known that I had it. Sometimes I almost wish that I had been born in one of the decent months. March, say.

ABOUT TERRY O'BRIEN

Terry O'Brien is an academic with three decades of experience in teaching language and communication skills in India and abroad. He also headed a college under the auspices of the University of Delhi.

A prolific writer, with several books to his credit, Terry O'Brien is a reputed professional motivational speaker and a quizmaster.